THE BARF OF THE BEDAZZLER

AARON REYNOLDS
Illustrated by Cam Kendell

Roaring Brook Press
New York

Published by Roaring Brook Press
Roaring Brook Press is a division of Holtzbrinck Publishing Holdings
Limited Partnership
120 Broadway, New York, NY 10271
mackids.com

Library of Congress Control Number: 2020912217
ISBN 978-1-250-20638-1

Our books may be purchased in bulk for promotional, educational, or business use. Please contact your local bookseller or the Macmillan Corporate and Premium Sales Department at (800) 221-7945 ext. 5442 or by email at MacmillanSpecialMarkets@macmillan.com.

First edition, 2021
Book design by Cassie Gonzales
Printed in the United States of America by LSC Communications,
Harrisonburg, Virginia

1   3   5   7   9   10   8   6   4   2

To Ed, Todd, and Jerod, my first band of merry
adventurers, for accompanying me to parts unknown
—A. R.

To Melissa, Max, Oscar, Virginia, and Charlie.
Thanks for all the flowers. *wink wink*
And to all of us on our own quests;
it's dangerous to go alone.
—C. K.

DWARVENFORGE
1

THE BRAMBLESHIRE
3

KARBUNKLE
EXPANSE
2

CENTRAL FEY
4

14

1

2

3

4

5

6

7

8

9

ISLE OF MOLAG
5

BLACKROOK
REACH
7

ELVEN KINGDOM
OF KIRAJOY
6

THE BARF OF THE
BEDAZZLER

Other books in the FART QUEST series

Fart Quest

CHAPTER ONE

We are totally surrounded.

The spindernots are closing in fast. And they out-number us ten to one.

SPINDERNOT

Disgusting.

Invades enchanted woods.

Gobbles up fairies and sprites.

Moxie, Pan, and I stand together. Warrior, monk, and mage. Dwarf, elf, and human. We form a triangle of awesomeness against these spidery foes.

I charge forward, ready to unleash my magic against these foul denizens of the forest. But some freaky unseen force holds me back. I am powerless! WHAT UNSPEAKABLE WITCHCRAFT IS AT WORK HERE?

"FART!" Pan calls to me. "Your robes are caught on that branch."

Oh. Apparently there is no unspeakable witchcraft at work here. Just a grabby tree.

I tug hard. The branch snaps free, sending me face-first into the dirt. I bump against Moxie. Who drops her hammer. Which falls on Pan's toe. Pan yowls in pain.

Dang. I was having such an empowering moment too.

My name is Fart.

Truth is, the three of us are not quite as mighty as I like to imagine. Really, we're just Level 2 heroes. Barely a step above newbie apprentices.

So where does that leave us? Oh, yeah.

We are totally surrounded.

Sensing our weakness, the spindernots have regrouped. Spinning a wall of webs, they slowly close in on us.

Things are not going according to plan, so Moxie does what Moxie does best. Takes action.

She pulls a small pouch from her belt. It's the magical bag of animal statues that she earned at the end of our last quest.

Gosh, I hope it does something cool.

She plucks a small figurine from the pouch and tosses it to the ground. It's a tiny hippo, meticulously carved and super adorable.

POOF! The figurine disappears and a full-size hippopotamus takes its place. The hippo lets out an earsplitting roar and charges the spindernots, sending them skittering for cover.

Yep. It does something cool.

The distraction buys me enough time to get to my feet.

I mentally run through the list of spells that I know:

FART'S SPELL LIST

 Gas Attack—My trademark spell

 Feather Friend—I can talk to birds

 Magic Missile—Shoots a flaming dart

 Puppy Power—Turns baddies into puppies

 Cozy Camp—Creates a small campfire. It's a baby spell, but perfect for the job right now.

"Flimmity-flamesh." A tiny magical fire sparks from my hands, burning away the closest webs.

Pan takes her cue. Using her monk ability to manipulate the elements, she sends the flames skittering across the webs, burning them away but carefully avoiding the trees. The last thing we want to do is torch the enchanted forest we were hired to protect.

We might not get paid. Plus Pan really loves trees.

Moxie's hippo tramples several spindernots and bashes into a tree, sending more spindernots scattering for cover. Moxie chases after it, twirling her hammer like a whirlwind.

KA-BLAMMO!

With one mighty swing, she sends six spindernots flying through the air.

Wow. Moxie's skills are getting impressive.

Pan snuffs out the flames, grabs her bo staff, and pole-vaults over the retreating spindernots. Doing a triple backflip, she lands and blocks their escape with her spinning staff.

Holy cow. I didn't know Pan could even do that.

A little niggle of jealousy rears up in me. Pan and Moxie are becoming super powerful. And I'm still casting my cute little Cozy Camp. I reach into my mind, trying to muster the words to the new spell I've been memorizing. It's time to show my friends that I can be impressive and amazing too.

I concentrate and mutter the magical words *"Plaintanitar au musa!"* Banana peels shoot from my palms. The spindernots slip. They slide.

The spindernots collapse in a heap. Moxie and the hippo leap upon them with abandon.

Dwarf hammer wallops. Hippo feet stomp.

KA-POW! KA-BLAM! KA-BLOOEY!

And, just like that, no more spindernots.

SUPERHEROIC ACHIEVEMENT!
Defeat a Horde of Spindernots!
(250 Experience Points Awarded)

Pan brushes dirt from her robes. "Nice work," she says. "Though I hesitate to point out that an enormous hippo and flying banana peels were not part of our carefully constructed plan."

Moxie shrugs. "What can I say? There were more spindernots than we thought. We had to improvise!"

The elf tucks her stray hair-wispies back into her topknot. "I am not a fan of improvisation."

"Aw, come on," says Moxie, shoving her playfully. "You're no fun."

"Fun?" says Pan. "I admit, fun is not my main priority."

"Speaking of fun improvisation," Moxie says,

shooting me a huge smile,
"Cute spell, banana brain! That
was hilarious!"

"Cute?" I cry. "Hilarious? Don't
you mean impressive? And amazing?" I step toward our conquered
foes, slip on a banana peel, and land
on my butt.

"Well, that *was* impressive," says
Pan with a smirk. "You only fell down
twice during that fight."

I flush with embarrass-
ment and chuck a banana

peel at her. She dodges it easily and yanks me to my feet.

With the spindernots vanquished, the magically summoned hippo nuzzles Moxie and disappears with a *POOF!*

Pan surveys the glade. "What a mess."

She's right. It looks like a gang of angry gnomes had a weeklong piñata party in this place.

It's not pretty. But we stand victorious.

And yet danger still lurks. Because we hear the fluttering of insect wings behind us.

We turn, hammer, staff, and spells at the ready.

But it's just our employer.

Ephemera. The pixie.

CHAPTER TWO

Ephemera claps her tiny hands
enthusiastically.

EPHEMERA

Loves giggling.

Hates spindernots.

Flower power!

"You did it!" Ephemera cries. "I was certain you would
meet your doom!"

"We get that a lot," Pan says.

"Such wee folk you are!" Ephemera cries.

"Did she just call us *wee*?" I ask. She's, like, four inches tall.

"But I thought, 'Give them a chance,'" the pixie says with a shrug.

"We're glad you did," I say.

"I thought, 'If they die, they die.'"

"Wait . . . what?" I look at Moxie.

"But you did it!" The pixie loops through the air in joy. "For you have vanquished the spindernots that plagued these fair woods. Once again, the Sparkly Grove shall be a haven of peace for the creatures of the forest!"

"We apologize for the mess," Pan says.

"Fear not," Ephemera says with a giggle. She produces a tiny wand and flutters around the grove, waving it merrily. Glittering dust drops to the forest floor.

The ground rustles. Quivers. Tufts of grass sprout, blotting all traces of the stampeding hippo. Vines shoot forth and blanket the fallen tree trunk, spindernots, and banana peels alike. Flowers bloom, leaving behind only green and white.

Bizzy, our giant bee companion, flutters around happily, poking her bumbly nose into the flowers.

Ephemera hovers over the trunk of the fallen tree. "It is always a tragedy when an ancient one falls to violence," the pixie says softly. "But life carries on!"

She slowly opens her hand. Her palm holds a tiny glowing speck. My ring of magic detection quivers in response. Whatever this thing is, it's magical. The pixie lovingly places the speck in the dirt. She covers it. A gentle stream of glistening water pours from the tip of her wand.

"Stand back," she whispers excitedly. "Watch what happens!"

We back away cautiously. The ground rumbles. The dirt churns. Suddenly an enormous tree shoots out of the ground. Leaves sprout. Branches soar. In a matter of seconds a colossal tree more than a hundred feet tall replaces the fallen one.

Canaries and robins emerge from the woods to nest in the new tree. Chipmunks scamper and titter from nearby grass tufts. All signs of our fight have disappeared. Pan sighs happily as neatness is restored around her.

Ephemera turns to us eagerly. "And now! Kneel and receive your reward, heroes!"

We kneel. She flits before us and bestows a soft kiss upon each of our foreheads.

SUPERHEROIC ACHIEVEMENT!
Kissed by a Pixie!
(200 Experience Points Awarded)

"For service to Ephemera of the Woods, I offer this small treasure." She waves her tiny wand. Three small pouches drop to the ground before us, tinkling with the sweet sound of gold nuggets.

Payment, as promised. We each grab a pouch and tuck it away. It would be rude to count it. Pixies are touchy like that.

"Now rise, friends of the Sparkly Grove," Ephemera coos. "The forest wishes to express its thanks."

Moxie looks at the trees uncertainly. "Um . . . you're welcome, forest."

"No, silly dwarf!" Ephemera giggles, fluttering to a landing on the end of Pan's bo staff. "Hold out your hand, fair monk," she whispers mischievously.

14

"A Seed of the Grove," the pixie whispers reverently. "Place it within fresh dirt. Water it! And stand back! A mighty titanfrond tree shall spread its roots and grow, bringing the peace of the Sparkly Grove to wherever you are!"

SUPERHEROIC ACHIEVEMENT!
Receive a Weird Magical Seed!
(200 Experience Points Awarded)

Pan bows solemnly. She unclasps the jade clip from her hair and snaps open the front, carefully placing the seed into the hidden compartment. She closes it with a *click*.

"Thank you, Ephemera," says Pan, returning the clip to her topknot.

"And now, farewell, my friends!" Ephemera zooms into the canopy and disappears from view. Just like that, she's gone.

I shake my pouch, enjoying the *clink-clink* of gold nuggets. "I like pixies. They pay in cash."

"And they know how to bring order from chaos," Pan says, looking around the tidy grove appreciatively. "Everything in its place, just as it should be."

Moxie grins and shoulders her shield and hammer. We follow her through the trees, leaving the Sparkly Grove behind us. Bizzy buzzes happily in our wake.

We soon emerge into the surrounding fields. Birds chirp. The late-summer sun sparkles playfully on Moxie's war hammer. The war hammer she inherited from Master Redmane. Her fingers run gently along the shining runes. "It's hard to believe it's only been a month," she says softly.

There's no need to say more. We nod quietly as we walk. One month ago, our masters died in a goblin attack gone horribly wrong.

Before that, we were students at Krakentop Academy for Heroes. When the time came for us to leave Krakentop, we followed our masters and began our hero wilderness training. We watched and learned. But deep down, we dreamed of doing our own daring deeds. That's when Master Redmane, Master Oonah, and Master Elmore were vaporized by goblin magic.

So be careful what you wish for.

The three of us had a big decision to make. Return to Krakentop in shame and disgrace? Or give this heroic adventurer thing a try on our own? You can guess which one we chose.

We were hired by the Great and Powerful Kevin to complete a mighty quest—the Quest for the Golden Lamia Fart. We fought ogres. Defeated an ettin. Vanquished a lamia. Got the fart. And saved a village.

Kevin rewarded us richly with some primo magical items.

MOXIE'S REWARD
Cool bag of magical animal figurines

PAN'S REWARD
Sassy Sandals of Silence

MY REWARD
Three spell scrolls, one-time use

Gold. Glory. And the adoration and appreciation of some very rustic villagers.

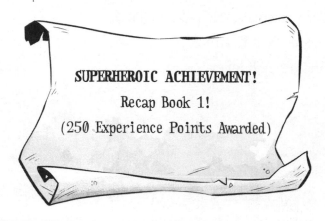

SUPERHEROIC ACHIEVEMENT!
Recap Book 1!
(250 Experience Points Awarded)

Not too shabby for three inexperienced apprentices.

And now here we are, just one month later. Pockets fat with gold nuggets. Getting hired by pixies. Kicking spindernot butt and taking spindernot names.

The sun is high when the town of Conklin comes into view. As we stroll into the quiet village, I stretch lazily and think about my bed at the Woozy Wyvern Inn. I'm ready for a well-earned nap.

But as we turn a corner, a shadow passes over the sun. Something lies in wait for us outside the inn.

It leaps on us. A creature from the darkest bogs. Slippery blue skin. Unblinking orange eyes.

19

Moxie turns to defend herself. But the creature has its slimy arms around her. And it squeezes.

And Moxie squeezes back.

For this creature is . . . a phibling.

His name is TickTock.

And he's a hugger.

CHAPTER THREE

His name is TickTock. And he's a hugger.

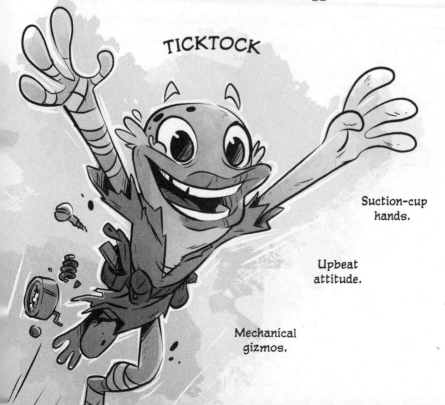

TICKTOCK

Suction-cup
hands.

Upbeat
attitude.

Mechanical
gizmos.

TickTock is the amphibian assistant to the Great and Powerful Kevin. On our last adventure, the little phibling proved to be inventive, resourceful, and a good friend.

"Hello, TickTock," says Pan, hugging the phibling warmly. "What are you doing here?"

"TickTock looks for Hammer-girl, elf-girl, and Fart-boy!" he cries. "The Great and Powerful Kevin is having a dangerous new quest. Is sending TickTock to get baby heroes!"

"I'm not really crazy about that term," I tell him with a sniff. "I just flung banana peels from my hands. Can a baby do that?"

"A baby monkey can," whispers Pan.

Moxie grins and turns to the phibling. "Well, lucky for Kevin, the baby heroes just finished up a job destroying a whole messload of spindernots."

Pan nods. "So I believe we are available."

As we follow the phibling, I have the eerie feeling that this quest is going to require all of our skill and power. I just hope I'm ready.

The Great and Powerful Kevin is waiting for us when we arrive. He pushes back the hood of his super-ominous robe. He locks onto us with his super-ominous eyes. He sets down his super-ominous lemonade. "What's up, dorks?"

"You tell us," says Pan, eyeing the tower and fidgeting with her necklace. "You called us here."

"What, no 'Hello'?" he asks, looking hurt. "No 'How have you been, Kevin'? No 'How's the family'?" He snorts and waves away the thought. "Straight to business, elf. I dig it."

Rising to his feet, he cracks his back and itches his ample tummy. "Come on inside," he says, squinting at Moxie's armor. "Your shininess is blinding me out here."

Kevin twirls dramatically and leads

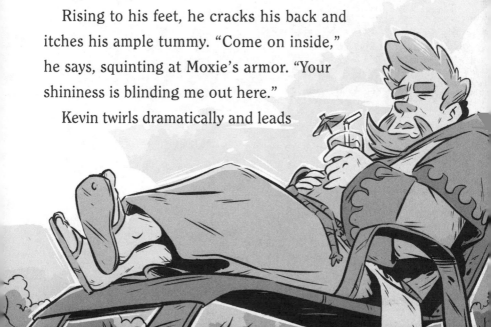

us into the tower. "I've got another quest that needs your heroic attention." We pass the front room full of TickTock's mechanical inventions. Go down a long hall. Around a dark corner. As we pass a staircase, a piercing voice echoes down from the rafters.

"KEVIN! WHO IS HERE?"

"Nobody!" he yells up the stairs. "Just some friends!"

"MAKE HASTE! YOU HAVE CHORES TO PERFORM!"

"Okay! Sheesh!"

He shakes his head in annoyance and leads us into a spooky chamber. Torches flicker dimly from the walls, casting long, eerie shadows across dozens of horrifying statues. Some are small. Some loom over us. But they are all statues of one thing.

Monsters.

"Oh my gosh!" says Moxie. "This is the coolest place I've ever seen!"

Of course it is. This girl has never met a creature covered in deadly teeth

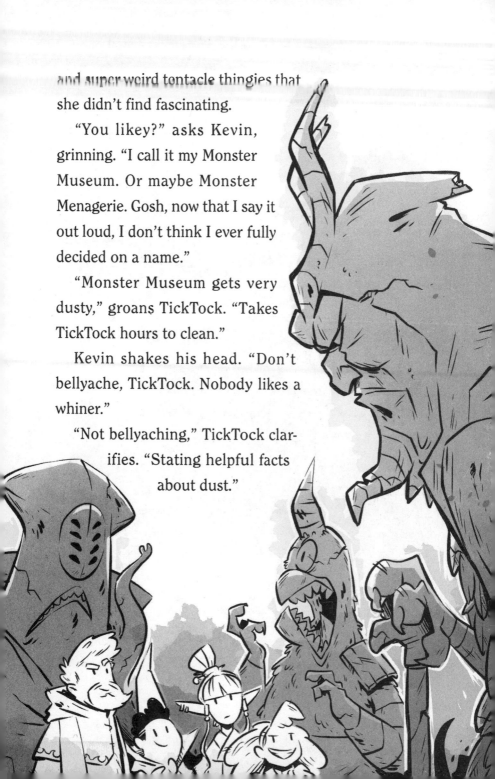

and super weird tentacle thingies that she didn't find fascinating.

"You likey?" asks Kevin, grinning. "I call it my Monster Museum. Or maybe Monster Menagerie. Gosh, now that I say it out loud, I don't think I ever fully decided on a name."

"Monster Museum gets very dusty," groans TickTock. "Takes TickTock hours to clean."

Kevin shakes his head. "Don't bellyache, TickTock. Nobody likes a whiner."

"Not bellyaching," TickTock clarifies. "Stating helpful facts about dust."

Moxie is already pulling out her favorite book: *Buzz-lock's Big Book of Beasts*.

"I know this," she says, pointing to a large statue of a bull-headed man. "That's a minotaur."

MINOTAUR

Lives in a labyrinth.

Hates bullfights. Also the color red.

"The shiny kid knows her stuff," says Kevin, nodding with approval.

Pan and I slowly roam among the still figures, taking them in. "What is this?" asks Pan, stopping before a skeletal figure.

Moxie thumbs through her book. "That's a lich," she says.

LICH

Powerful undead mage.

Most weapons have no effect.

Soul Silo: an object that contains a lich's soul. (Weakens the lich if you take it.)

Buzzlock's advice: Run.

"Gross." I gulp at the thought of bumping into a lich in a dark alley.

"Don't worry," says Kevin. "I didn't call you here to talk about minotaurs or liches."

He leads us over to a dark alcove. Something stands in the shadows, covered with a silk cloth. I shiver in anticipation. Whatever is under there is going to be bad news.

"I called you here for this," he says, whipping off the cloth.

Gulp. Double gulp. There are lots of horrible monsters in this room. But this one's the worst.

"I think I like the lich better," I whimper.

"Smart kid," says Kevin. "Do you know what this is?"

"It's a bedazzler," says Moxie.

"Exactly!" says Kevin, looking impressed. "You're pretty bright for a warrior. What can you tell me about bedazzlers?"

Moxie pulls her gaze away from the statue and flips her book to the *B* section. She begins to read aloud.

BEDAZZLER

Huge eye shields it from magic.

Very rare.

Gemstones shoot beams of power like sleep, petrification, and even disintegration.

"Nicely done, Bright-and-Shiny," says Kevin. He turns his gaze to each of us in turn. "Information on bedazzlers is a little sketchy. Most people who encounter them don't continue breathing long enough to share the gory details."

"Oookay . . ." I turn nervously back to the statue. "So these bedazzlers are super bad and horrible."

"You got that right," says Kevin. "You would not want to get anywhere close to one of these dudes."

"So," says Pan, crossing her arms, "what does this have to do with us?"

Kevin pulls back his hood. "I need you to get really close to one of these dudes," he says. "I need you to find me a bedazzler."

CHAPTER FOUR

"Have you lost your great and powerful mind?" I cry.

"You dweebs wanted a quest!" says Kevin. "This is a quest!"

"No!" cries TickTock, pulling on Kevin's robes. "Bedazzler statue once make TickTock accidentally pee himself while dusting. Kevin cannot be sending them to be fighting a real one! Too dangerous!"

Moxie squeezes the handle of her war hammer. "This is one major-league baddie. Check out all those teeth."

"This *is* quite unexpected," says Pan. "Trying to slay this creature would spell certain doom for even seasoned heroes. And while we have accomplished some admirable tasks, we are fairly unseasoned."

Kevin shakes his head. "You noobs need to turn on your listening ears. Did I say anything about *slaying* a bedazzler?"

Pan quirks an eyebrow at Kevin. "I believe you asked us to find you a bedazzler."

"Yeah," says Kevin. "Find! Not slay. You'd never survive a battle against a bedazzler! You guys are barely out of preschool!"

"Then please explain," says Pan. "What is it you want us to do?

"Find a bedazzler!" says Kevin. "And bring me something back."

I'm afraid to ask. "Bring back what?"

Kevin turns away from us and mumbles something. It sounds like *brf*.

"We can't understand you," I say.

"Barf!" cries Kevin, turning around. "Okay? GOSH!"

"What in the name of the Fourteen Realms do you need with bedazzler barf?" asks Moxie.

"Don't worry about it," says Kevin. "You kids wouldn't understand it even if I told you. All you need to know is that I require bedazzler barf for some very cool magical stuff I'm doing."

I grab a fistful of my robes. "And how are we supposed to get bedazzler barf without slaying one?" I ask.

"Don't ask me!" Kevin cries. "You dudes are the heroes! I imagine you're going to have to put on your thinking caps and come up with a plan."

"Yes," Pan says, nodding in agreement. "A foolproof plan will be critical."

"But don't try to slay it," Kevin reminds us. "Because then you'll be dead. And I'll have to find some other heroes to run my errands. And that would be incredibly inconvenient for me."

"Let's burn that bridge when we get to it," says Moxie. "But we still have a problem."

"You're a bunch of gutless fraidy-cats?"

"No."

"What, then?"

Moxie looks thoughtfully over the page of her book. "It says here that bedazzlers are very rare." She turns her gaze on Kevin. "Where are we going to find one?"

"Now that's something I *can* help you with," Kevin says, a smarmy grin spreading across his face. "Rumor has it there's one man alive who knows the whereabouts of a living, breathing bedazzler."

I clap my hands together. "Easy-peasy," I say. "We

find this guy. Smack him around. Get him to tell us where the bedazzler is."

Kevin shakes his shaggy head. "Not so easy. And not so peasy. This guy isn't just a guy. He's Diremaw the Dread. The pirate."

"Diremaw the Dread?" Moxie gasps in awe.

"You know of this man?" asks Pan.

Moxie gulps. "When I was an orphan on the streets of Sludgebottom, kids used to tell scary stories about him. They say he can hypnotize you just by looking at you. They say he can peer directly into your soul and read your every thought!"

"Well, I don't know about all that stuff," says Kevin. "But Diremaw the Dread is definitely one bad dude."

"He takes no prisoners. Leaves nobody alive. If he attacks your ship on the high seas, you're pretty much toast."

"So what does he look like?" I ask.

"Dunno," Kevin says with a shrug. "Nobody but his crew has ever seen him."

"So," says Pan. "If you've never seen this pirate captain, where are we supposed to find him?"

Kevin pulls a parchment from the sleeve of his robe and unfurls it.

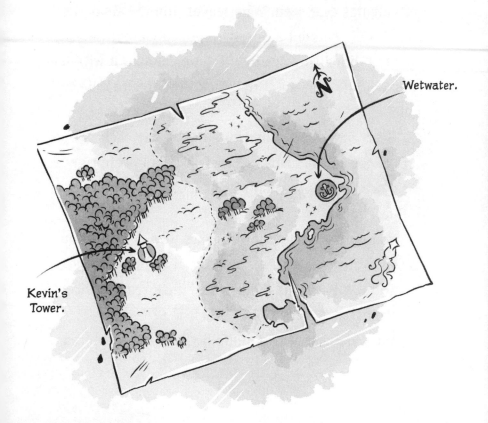

Wetwater.

Kevin's Tower.

"This"—he points to the map—"is the harbor city of Wetwater. It is filthy. Crime-ridden. And dangerous. You'll love it."

Pan covers her face and groans.

"Rumor has it that Diremaw's ship, the *Death Knell*, always makes harbor there this time of year," Kevin says, grinning behind his goatee. "He'll need to resupply. Maybe take on more crew. So he can do one more round of pirating before winter sets in."

"Awesome," I say. "Go to Wetwater. Find a pirate nobody has ever seen. Who leaves nobody alive. Get him to tell us about a horrifying deadly creature. Go find that horrifying deadly creature. Hang out with it long enough to make it upchuck. And live to tell the tale."

"See?" says Kevin, smacking me on the back. "You totally get it!" He turns to TickTock. "You were right, TickTock. He's not as doofy as he looks."

I feel queasy.

"You guys will figure it out!" says Kevin. "When you get to Wetwater, look up an old pal of mine. Magda Rumrunner. She owns an inn called the Fried Phoenix."

"Well, that at least sounds promising," I say.

Pan shakes her head doubtfully. "I am not convinced.

This quest is quite dangerous and complicated." She eyeballs Kevin skeptically. "Why should we take this on?"

"Because you will be amply rewarded," says Kevin. He tosses a small sack into my hands. "With a bonus up front."

I feel the weight in my hands. I hear the *clink-clink* of gold coins. At least five hundred of them.

"So what do you say?" asks Kevin. "Will you dweebs take on my quest?"

"Are you kidding?" says Moxie. "Go get some weird bodily function from some horrific creature with little to no hope of returning alive?" Her face splits into a wide grin. "Sounds amazing!"

She turns to me.

I grit my teeth. "It makes me nervous. But if we're going to be heroes, I guess we're going to have to keep doing heroic things."

Moxie and I both turn to Pan. Her face is set like stone.

Kevin huffs impatiently. He leans over to me. "Whatcha think?" he hisses. "Should I slap a Mind Control spell on her so we can move things along here?"

"Mind Control?" I shake my head at him. "I've never heard of that spell."

"Of course not, little magic dude. You're still a baby."

I grit my teeth in aggravation. I'm really starting to hate that word.

"What's it gonna be, sister?" Kevin asks Pan.

She lets out a long sigh. "There was a time when my life was neat and orderly," she says softly. "I miss those days."

She looks to us. She takes a deep breath. And she finally turns to Kevin. "We'll do it," she says. "On one condition."

Kevin's face splits into a grin. "Name it."

"You send TickTock along with us."

TickTock's mouth drops open and stays there. "You want TickTock to go?"

"Heck yeah!" cries Moxie.

Pan raises an eyebrow at Kevin. "TickTock has proven himself talented, loyal, and resourceful. But more than that, he is our friend."

The phibling sputters something in Phibish, but I can't make it out because he's starting to blubber.

"Whoa," says Kevin. "Hold on there, Nelly. Tick-Tock is my number one helper-dude. If he goes with you, who's going to build my gadgets? Who's going to assist me in my experiments? And, most important, who's going to make my breakfast? That phibling knows exactly how I like my eggs."

Runny yolk.

Crispy whites.

Ketchup.

Hash browns
on the side.

Pan crosses her arms. "How badly do you want your barf?"

Kevin lets out a loud groan. "Fine," he says. "I guess I can have toast for breakfast until you get back."

Pan plucks the map from Kevin's hands with a smirk.

"Pack your bags, everyone," she says, cocking a long, pointy eyebrow at us. "It looks like we're going to Wetwater."

CHAPTER FIVE

The quickest way to Wetwater is straight through a smelly, disgusting swamp.

So, of course, that's where we are. Staring out at Blight Bog Funk.

"Yuck," says TickTock.

"Yuck?" asks Moxie. "You're a phibling. Aren't you supposed to like swamps and mud and stuff?"

"TickTock is liking things that go *click* and *clack* and *tick* and *tock*. Why are you thinking TickTock's clan is making him leave phibling village?"

Huh. I guess I'm not the only one who got kicked out of his family.

Bizzy flutters nervously at my side. I don't blame her. A nasty swamp sprawls before us. A deadly quest lies beyond that. But I'm too distracted to be nervous. Because one word just keeps rolling through my mind.

Baby.

I am sick and tired of hearing that word!

Trouble is . . . Kevin and TickTock are right. Ever since our last adventure, Moxie is walloping six baddies at a time and Pan is leaping higher and flying farther than I ever knew she could.

Me? Still doing baby spells.

I reach for the fat spellbook hanging at my side. I thumb through the well-worn pages at the beginning of the book. The place where all the starter spells live.

Master Elmore always said that the key to building power was one little step at a time. Start with the basics and work up to the hard stuff. But it's time to seriously up my game. My finger moves to the smoother, less-used pages at the back of the book. The place where the advanced magic is. Maybe it's time to skip over a few chapters and show everybody that I'm not the infant they think I am.

KER-SQUISH!

My thoughts fade away like a frog. Because Moxie has just plunged waist-deep into the sludge, splattering me with muck in the process. I tuck my spellbook under my robes to protect it from swamp slime.

"We'll never get across this!" Moxie cries, tugging herself out of the muck.

"I agree," Pan says, nose wrinkled in distaste. "This is going to be one very messy journey."

"Not if you listen to TickTock!" says the phibling.

Stepping only where TickTock is doing steps.

"Nicely done, TickTock," says Pan approvingly, following in his footsteps. "I thought you hated swamps."

"TickTock does," says the phibling thoughtfully.

"But TickTock guesses he is still being a phibling. Some things are being part of you always."

The deeper we go, the murkier it gets. Deformed trees reach out of the sludge like skeleton fingers, grasping at us. Wet slimy things ripple in the water nearby. Thankfully nothing ventures too close, except the bugs, which are eating us alive.

The minutes turn to hours, and still we tromp through the sludge. I'm cold. I'm wet. I think I have the sniffles.

"Look at that," says Moxie, pointing.

Hanging from a nearby tree is a carving. Pan looks closely at the symbol. "This is a carving of a stank frond. It's some sort of territorial marker. Something has claimed this area as its domain."

"Probably something horribly evil," says Moxie. "With ten legs and lots of teeth."

"We must move cautiously from here," whispers Pan. We slip past the marker and keep trudging into the mist.

Pan says we're still heading in roughly the right direction. I have no idea how she knows this, but since elves are all in touch with nature and directions and the moon and junk, I'll take her word for it.

Then, just when I'm about to go completely insane from boredom and wet socks, we see it.

A little ball of light. Blinking. Dancing in the distance.

Then another little light winks into view.

Then a third. They hover tauntingly. Beckoning us.

To safety.

Or to a grisly doom.

CHAPTER SIX

An eerie chill runs through me that has nothing to do with gooey socks. "Somebody tell me you see those lights," I say.

"I see them," says Pan, squinting through the mist. "Put out the torch."

I drop the flame into the muck, and it sputters out with a hiss. But still, the balls of light blink and bob in the distance, like creepy eyes playing peekaboo.

"Oh crud," says Moxie. "I know what these are."

"Friendly helpful people with lanterns?" says Tick-Tock. "Is that what Hammer-girl is going to be saying?"

"Nope," she says grimly. "That's what they want you to think. But they're really wisp wraiths."

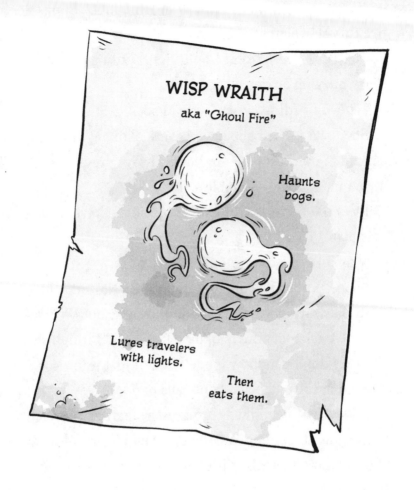

WISP WRAITH

aka "Ghoul Fire"

Haunts bogs.

Lures travelers with lights.

Then eats them.

I'm wet. I'm slimy. I'm lost in a bog. And now evil balls of light are waving at us. Cool.

"TickTock," says Pan. "See if you can find a path that leads away from the lights."

"Going away from the creepy death lights." I nod. "I like this new plan very much."

TickTock veers right. I hold tightly to Pan's robes, Bizzy buzzing anxiously at my side.

"They're getting closer," says Moxie.

She's right. The bobbing lights are blinking furiously, closing in on their prey. And when I say "prey," I mean my plump and highly edible self.

I feel the hysteria taking over inside me. "We need a new plan," I say.

"I am open to suggestions," says Pan.

"Good, 'cause I've got one," I cry. "RUN!"

It's like saying it aloud trips off the panic button in all of us. We dart forward, slopping furiously through the sludge. I don't care how muddy I get. I just want to get away from the diabolical light balls of doom.

Suddenly I'm yanked into the air, feetfirst. I reach out to grab something. Anything. My hands find Moxie's shield. Pan's nose. But it's not the wisp wraiths that have us.

We've all been snatched up by a giant net.

"Gotta get out!" I scream in panic. "Gotta get out!"

Only nothing devours us. Instead we hear a sound. The first sound I've heard all day. Besides the bugs.

And my own screaming.

It's the unmistakable sound of bowstrings being drawn.

"Now that there's a fine idea," says a voice. "Git out while the gittin's good. Only exceptin' you is on our land. So you ain't gittin' nowhere."

As the net slowly spins, I see . . . a dozen dark figures surrounding us.

"Cut 'em down, Jethro," says the voice from the shadows.

SHWICK!

We clatter to the muck in a jumble of legs and robes and weapons. Moxie is on her feet instantly, hammer in hand.

The bobbing lights shine in our eyes. But they suddenly seem a lot less ghostly.

"Moxie," I hiss. "I don't think these are wisp wraiths!"

I hear whoops of laughter from all around us.

"Jethro, I do declare!" says the voice. "That wisp

wraith trick is the finest idea you ever had. Next time I find me a stank frond, I'm fixin' to give you the whole thing. You earned it!"

"Thank ye kindly, Peat Blossom!" says Jethro.

I turn to Moxie. "Trick?"

"Yes, indeedy," hoots the one called Peat Blossom. "A right fine one too! Now y'all best be dropping them weapons. Lest ya wanna get pincushioned full of arrows!"

Moxie grips and ungrips her hammer. I know the look on her face. She has no plans to drop her hammer. She's about to charge into battle like a rampaging hippo.

"Why don't you lower those lights?" she shouts. "So we can get a good look at your cowardly faces!"

Peat Blossom snaps her fingers. At her signal, the dark figures lower their lanterns, revealing the faces that circle us. Their upturned eyes. Their long eyebrows.

And their delicate pointy ears.

We are completely surrounded.

By elves.

CHAPTER SEVEN

"Last warning," says Peat Blossom. "You got to the count of three to drop 'em."

Moxie raises her shield, ready to attack. But, unexpectedly, Pan steps forward and lays her bo staff on the ground.

Moxie whirls on her. "What are you doing?"

"One!"

Pan reaches over and puts a hand on Moxie arm. "Do it," she says.

"Why would I do that?"

"Because, Moxie," Pan says. "Look at them."

Moxie turns to the figures before us. Bows drawn. Faces stern.

"Two!" says Peat Blossom.

"They're elves," Pan says. "Like me." She lowers Moxie's hammer arm.

Moxie grits her teeth. But she drops her hammer into the muck. I drop my staff. TickTock tosses his dagger. Bizzy even tucks away her stinger.

"Smart move, y'all," says Peat Blossom.

Pan holds out her palms and strides confidently toward the lead elf.

"Thelasma au delnadre enenthau Panalathalasas," says Pan.

Peat Blossom squints at her. "What'd you say to me, runt?"

"Sentau aureanth ethenousenlasa?" says Pan.

"You best shut that jibber-jabber up right quick," says Peat Blossom. "Before you get yerself hurt."

Pan crosses her arms. "That is not jibber-jabber," she says. "That is High Elvish. I would expect any elf to understand it."

"Well, la-dee-da, Yer Highness," says Peat Blossom with a laugh. "Hear that, y'all? That there's High Elvish! Any elf worth spit should be able to understand it!"

The elves burst into laughter.

Peat Blossom leans in close to Pan. "We ain't high elves, sweetheart." She takes off her hat and flicks some moss from it. Her hat is tattered, but her eyes are full of fire. "We're muck elves."

Peat Blossom shoves Pan with the tip of her bow. "Now scootch back on over next to yer friends. And no more talkin'."

"I thought they were elves," Moxie whispers. "Like you."

"They may be elves," says Pan, wrinkling her nose in distaste, "but they are nothing like me."

Peat Blossom turns to her companions. "Know what, boys?"

"What's that, Peat Blossom?"

"Since princess here can't keep her yap shut, let's

just simplify things good and proper." Peat Blossom pulls out a small tube. A blowgun. "Dart 'em."

FFFT! FFFT! FFFT! FFFT!

I feel a prick in my neck. Drowsiness hits me hard, and I know I've just been shot with a sleeping dart.

CHAPTER EIGHT

When I wake up, I've got a weird feeling. It's that feeling of dangling from a pole like a feast-day goose. You know the one.

I open my eyes. And I realize why I feel that way.

'Cause I'm in a boat, dangling from a pole like a feast-day goose.

"Where are you taking us?" I demand. Only I'm still kinda groggy. So it comes out mostly as "Wherakaboo?"

"Ain't takin' you nowhere," says Peat Blossom. "We're here."

These weird elves don't speak High Elvish. But apparently they speak Wherakaboo.

"Welcome," says Peat Blossom, "to the Holler."

I don't know what a holler is. But what I see knocks my socks off. My wet, soggy socks.

The boat drifts to a stop under a large building. Peat Blossom lets out a call, and suddenly we're rising up into the belly of the building.

We are led through dim halls to a thick wooden door. The elves throw us in. And lock the door.

"Y'all get good and comfy, now," Peat Blossom hoots through the bars in the tiny window. She glares at Pan. "Especially

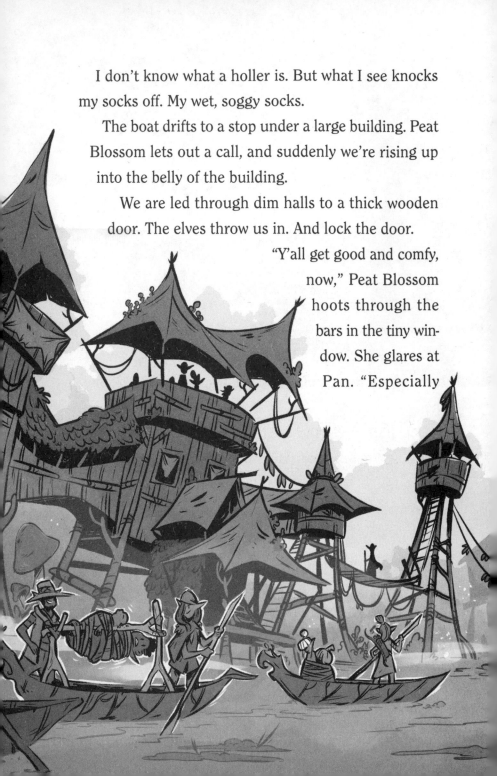

you, precious. After all, this here's the luxury suite. Reserved especially for the use of high elves like you!"

She lets out a laugh and ambles away. Two elves with spears take up positions outside the door. And there's silence. Just the hum of crickets and swamp frogs fills the air.

"This is great," says Moxie. "Just great." She turns to Pan. "We should have fought them when we had the chance!"

"These are not spindernots," says Pan. "These are elves."

"And I'm a dwarf!"

"They had bows," Pan points out.

"I have a hammer!"

Wrong. HAD a hammer.

All our weapons have been taken.

"I understand how you feel," Pan says, shaking her head in exasperation. "They took my necklace. That belonged to my mother!" She flops into a dark corner. "But they would have shot us down before we even landed one hit."

"At least we would have gone down fighting!" Moxie snaps.

"Fighting a group of elves is never a logical choice," Pan says. "Even reckless, slovenly elves like these."

"Yeah," Moxie mumbles. "Because getting locked in jail is real logical."

I hate seeing Moxie like this. "It's not Pan's fault," I remind her.

Moxie whirls on me. "NOW you chime in?"

"What did I do?"

"Nothing!" she cries. "That's the problem!"

"Now wait just a second . . ." I start.

"I'm Fart!" Moxie says mockingly, doing a completely terrible imitation of my voice. "When danger strikes, I stand there and say nothing. Or I cast Banana-Pants!"

"That spell is called Slip 'N Slide," I inform her. "And for the record, you sound nothing like me!"

"I sound exactly like you."

"NOTHING!" I screech.

"Friends! Stop fighting with our own selves!" Tick-Tock yells.

Moxie lets out a long sigh. She looks at me sheepishly. "Sorry." She grips and ungrips the bars and then huddles miserably in a dark corner.

I sigh in helpless defeat. She's not wrong. I could never take action the way Moxie does. She would brave a hundred minotaurs with nothing but her hammer and a spunky attitude. She'd body-slam a thousand liches, and the smile would never leave her face. But being locked up like this . . . Without her shield. Without her hammer. It's gotta be pure torture.

TickTock wrings his hands and shivers next to me. "TickTock and swamps always be a bad idea."

I flump down next to the phibling. "So you had to leave your home too?"

TickTock looks up at me. "Yes. Phiblings are not believing in metal and machines. Are saying it is unnatural. TickTock broke phibling laws by building his gizmos. Phiblings say TickTock is no phibling. Banish him from the swamp forever. Say never come back."

"Wow," I whisper. "I get it."

"This is the same for Fart-boy?" asks TickTock.

"Let's just say I was not a great farmer."

TickTock sighs and curls into a ball. "TickTock likes Fart-boy, whether good farmer or not. But now that TickTock is in a muck-elf prison, he is wishing baby heroes had left TickTock with Kevin."

There's that word again. I've had it with being a baby hero. I'm ready for monsters and muck elves and even Pan and Moxie to look at me with trembling awe!

My staff and dagger are gone. But there . . . hidden

60

underneath my robes. I feel my spellbook. Clearly the elves missed it when they confiscated all our weapons.

I flop the heavy book onto my lap. I thumb through the pages. Past the well-worn first-level spells. Past the dog-eared intermediate spells. To the back of the book.

Here the pages are smooth and unstained. Here the spells have powerful and mysterious names.

Meteor Storm
Merlin's Gurgling Squirt
Mind Control

Mind Control. It's the spell Kevin mentioned. I try to imagine the possibilities that would be at my fingertips if I had the power to control the thoughts and actions of the muck elves.

It's fun to imagine. But I can already hear Master Elmore's voice in my head. *Don't get ahead of yourself, boy! You're not ready for that! Think small!*

And yet. Where did that kind of thinking get Master Elmore? Dead. Kaput. Killed by goblins.

That's where.

CHAPTER NINE

It's impossible to know how long we've been rotting away in this cell.

Days?

Weeks?

Months?

At long last, we hear the rattle of keys.

It's Peat Blossom. "Wakey-wakey, eggs and bakey," she says. "Only without the bakey. And no eggs, either."

"It's about time!" I cry. This endless imprisonment has broken my spirit completely. I'll do whatever they say. I'll tell them anything they want to know.

"Whatcha mean 'about time'?" Peat Blossom asks. "Y'all only been in here about twenty minutes."

Oh.

"Now git up," she says, unlocking the door. "Y'all been summoned."

"Summoned?" asks Moxie. "By who?"

"By the madam of the muck. The soul of the sludge. The head honcho of the Holler." Peat Blossom smiles broadly. "Y'all been summoned by the Grand High Meemaw."

We are led to a great hall. The ceiling is ribbed, like the underside of a giant mushroom. Glowing beetles and iridescent lizards bathe the room with radiance. It is otherworldly and magnificent. But before us sits the most otherworldly and magnificent sight of all.

Her golden skin reflects the oranges, purples, and

blues of the lights around us. Yet it seems to glow with a source of its own.

I kneel.

"Stand, child," she says. Her voice is rich and deep. "There's no need for that here."

She takes a moment and looks at each of us in turn.

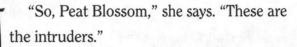

"So, Peat Blossom," she says. "These are the intruders."

"Yes, Meemaw," says Peat Blossom. "We found 'em trompin' through our lands like they owned the place."

Moxie steps forward. "Excuse me, Your Majesty."

"Please, child. Call me Meemaw."

"Well, Meemaw," she says, scratching her armpit awkwardly. "We were just traveling through your swamp on our way to the city of Wetwater. We didn't mean to trespass."

"We muck elves are a territorial bunch," Meemaw says melodiously. "We love our home and we guard her borders well. It is not our rule to welcome outsiders freely."

Moxie gulps. "We didn't know."

"I wonder," says Meemaw. "Is ignorance of a rule an

excuse to break it?" She turns her head to address Pan. "What do you say to this, *Panalathalasas*?"

Pan's ears perk up at the use of her proper elvish name.

She eyes the woman thoughtfully, as if weighing her response. I cringe. She has not been impressed with these odd elves. Showing disrespect to their boss lady could be bad news for all of us.

"No, it is not," says Pan softly. "We saw the markers. We should have sought permission before entering these lands. We are guilty."

Moxie drops her head into her hands. Pan has sealed our doom.

But Meemaw seems satisfied with this answer. She squints down at us, evaluating us carefully.

"I sense no malice in your hearts. I believe that you meant us no harm or intrusion."

"That's right!" says TickTock. "No intrusion was being meant! Not even a little—"

"Yet intrude you did," whispers Meemaw, cutting the phibling short. "Therefore, as payment for your uninvited trespass, you will perform a small act of service for us."

Pan looks around at the muck elves who stand in

neat formation before their leader. She kneels in respect. "We accept this judgment."

"Beg pardon, Meemaw," interrupts Peat Blossom. "Yer gonna let this riffraff off with a slap on the wrist? You shoulda heard how this fancy-pants elf talked to us! On our own lands!"

"Peace, Peat Blossom," says Meemaw. "This is no slap on the wrist, child."

The Grand High Meemaw stands. Colorful beads rattle at her neck and her housecoat flows softly around her feet.

"They will vanquish SquishRabble from our lands once and for all. In doing so, they will earn our respect, our friendship, and their freedom."

SUPERHEROIC ACHIEVEMENT!
Get a Quest within a Quest!
(100 Experience Points Awarded)

Peat Blossom rubs her grimy hands together. "Yer sendin' them to fight SquishRabble?" She shoots a look at Pan. "Oh boy. This is gonna be good!"

Meemaw holds up her hand. "Do not rejoice yet, Peat Blossom. Because you are going to lead them there."

CHAPTER TEN

We've been given our weapons back. Moxie hugs her hammer like she's never letting go.

Meemaw promises our gold and other possessions will be returned if we slay SquishRabble. Which, according to Peat Blossom, doesn't seem likely.

Though with a name like SquishRabble, how scary can he be?

Peat Blossom chooses two more muck elves to escort us. Jethro. And some guy named Boondoggle.

After a couple hours hiking through the sludge, Peat Blossom calls for a stop.

"We'll rest here, y'all," she says. She makes herself comfy on a filthy log and pulls out a musical instrument.

"Music?" Moxie grips and ungrips her hammer nervously. "You sure that's a good idea? You might attract something yucky."

"Trust me," she says. "I know these parts better'n the back of my hand. A little fiddle-playin' is safe fer now."

Jethro pulls out a harmonica and Boondoggle grabs some sort of reed flute from his pack.

"Oh goody," Pan whispers. "Prepare yourselves for a down-home jamboree."

Peat Blossom lowers her fiddle. "Yer a snob, princess."

"My name is *Panalathalasas*, not princess," says Pan curtly. "If you must call me anything, call me Pan."

Pan looks for a clean spot to sit, but everywhere is moist and mucky. "And no, I'm not a snob. I was just taught how to be an elf."

Rational.
Methodical.
Logical.
Clean.

Peat Blossom looks at her quietly for a moment. "Well, maybe you shouldn't judge people so quick. Maybe"—she pauses to spit a loogie into the sludge nearby—"just maybe there's more'n one way to be an elf."

She raises the bow to her fiddle and plays. As Jethro and Boondoggle join in, the melody rises into the night sky. I've never heard anything like it. If soaring eagles and dancing fireflies and thunderstorms gathering on the horizon could be turned into music, this is what it would sound like.

I don't know how much time passes. Minutes? An hour? But when they are done playing, I glance at Pan. She's wiping her eyes with her sleeve. Nobody dares to breathe as the spell of the music fades into the night.

Pan finally plops down in the muck moss with a *squelch*. "Why must everything in this place be so filthy?"

Peat Blossom shoots a look at Pan. "Ain't you a monk?"

"Yes."

"Ain't monks supposed to be all lovey-dovey fer the elements?"

"I suppose."

"And ain't earth and water two of them elements?"

"Yes. Yes, they are."

"So what's more glorious than bein' covered in muck, which is just earth and water mixed together?"

Pan clears her throat uncomfortably. "I guess I never thought of that."

An awkward silence descends. TickTock clears his throat. "TickTock has never heard of elves living in swamps."

"Yeah, me neither," chimes in Moxie. "Why do you live on this mucky land?"

"That there's a long story," says Peat Blossom. "And one that ain't really yer business, if we're bein' honest. But we done made it our home. And we come to love it."

And ain't nobody gonna ever take our home away from us again.

Pointy
Point
Point

"I never thought of that, either," says Pan softly.

"There's a lot you ain't never thought of," says Peat Blossom. The muck elves shoulder their packs and rise wordlessly. "Let's move. Ain't got too far to go. It's time fer y'all to meet SquishRabble."

CHAPTER ELEVEN

An enormous deformed tree claws the sky before us.

Jethro and Boondoggle eye the tree in terror. But Peat Blossom is cucumber-cool.

"That there's SquishRabble," whispers Peat Blossom, pointing at the tree.

The tree looks super haunted and long dead, but other than that it just looks like a tree. "I don't see anything," I hiss.

But Moxie points up into the branches.

And there, as the moon peeks out from behind a cloud, I see it. A creature wrapped in a cocoon of vines and twigs.

Oh my gosh. SquishRabble is a big boy.

SQUISHRABBLE

Super squishy.

Needs serious manscaping.

So . . . many . . . mouths.

"Good luck," says Jethro. The elves turn and head into the mist.

"Whoa, whoa, whoa!" says Moxie. "Aren't you gonna give us any pointers?"

"You gotta whoop him fast," says Peat Blossom. "'Cuz he'll start sendin' off spores. And if them things take root, yer gonna have more than one muck man on yer hands. Yer gonna have one big daddy muck man and a messload of little baby muck men."

"Say 'muck man' a few more times," I tell her. "I don't think I've got the full picture."

Pan eyes the muck elves suspiciously. "You seem like skilled fighters."

"Yes indeedy," Boondoggle answers without hesitation. "We beat you."

Moxie grins. "Well, we never technically fought," she argues.

"But my point is," Pan interrupts, "why haven't you simply taken care of this muck man yourselves?"

Peat Blossom gives Pan a calculating look. "'Cuz muck elves got sensitive ears," she answers. "I'm guessing your hearing is less touchy on account of that thick head of yours." Peat Blossom tugs some oversize earmuffs from her pack. She hands them to Pan. "Just in case, you better put these on, high elf."

"Why?" asks Pan, taking the earmuffs nervously.

"On account of the screeching," says Jethro.

"Good luck," says Peat Blossom again. "We'll keep watch from over here." And they disappear into the mist.

We turn and face the decrepit tree. "Well, we clearly need a plan," Pan points out.

"We could do the old standby," suggests Moxie.

"What's that?" I ask.

"I beat it on the head with my hammer until it stops moving."

"What about the spores?" Pan asks.

"Oh, yeah," I say. "Unless you can conk it out in one shot, it's going to be muck-baby city around here."

"TickTock knows!" chirps the phibling. "Fart-boy can be using Gas Attack on it!"

"Brilliant idea, TickTock." Pan nods. "Great plan."

"How is that a great plan?" I hiss. "I'd have to be touching him. I'm a terrible climber! There's no way I can get up there."

Bizzy nuzzles me nervously. I look at her, fluttering noiselessly beside me.

Or can I?

I have never ridden a giant bumblebee. I'm guessing
you haven't either. Allow me to be the first to tell you . . .
it's a wobbly ride.

We're twenty feet from SquishRabble. Ten feet. Five.

All I have to do is reach out and touch the muck
man, say the magic incantation, and *POOF!* He'll be a
harmless gas cloud.

SNICK!

And then his eyes pop open. He snorts, spots us, and snatches us right out of the air. Being in his mucky veggie fist is not how I envisioned touching him, but it'll do. I open my mouth to say the words of my Gas Attack spell—

And vines shoot from his hand, entwining my head. My throat. And my mouth.

Crud on a cracker. I'm gagged. If I can't spit words out of my word hole, I can't do magic.

SquishRabble leaps from the treetop, landing with a mighty *squelch*. He glares at my friends. And he lets out a silent roar from his many monstrous mouths.

Pan crumples to the floor.

"What's wrong?" Moxie cries, eyeing the muck man.

"TickTock is hearing nothing," the phibling shouts. "But TickTock is seeing a giant muck-man fist coming our way!"

Moxie, Pan, and TickTock scatter as the muck man beats the earth with his free fist.

"It must be an elf thing!" Pan yells. She's trying to grit through it. But it's clear that her pain is excruciating. "I can't stay. I'm sorry!" Hands over ears, she dashes into the mist.

Moxie and TickTock turn back to see me and Bizzy trapped in SquishRabble's fist of fronds. Without hesitation they bravely charge to our rescue, swinging their weapons heroically.

But it's like trying to beat up a veggie stir-fry.

SQUELCH! SQUISH! SQUASH!

Small glowing puffballs leak from his body and float to the swampy ground. At first I think maybe he's bleeding plant-man puffball blood. But then I realize.

He's releasing spores.

Moxie swings. TickTock stabs.

It does nothing but annoy the muck man. Which makes him squeeze Bizzy and me even harder.

The tightening vines cut off my air. I'm starting to see stars. And I realize this is how things end for me.

Squashed to death by a salad.

CHAPTER TWELVE

Things are going dark.

It's all over. I'm done for.

And that's when I see Peat
Blossom. And Jethro. And Boondoggle.

Flying.

The muck elves seem caught up in an invisible
tornado. They spiral through the air, sending a shower
of arrows at me. No. At SquishRabble.

THWICK! THWACK! THWUCK!

Arrows squelch into SquishRabble's face. Their
furious barrage of arrows is definitely distract-
ing him. He holds out his hands to shield his

face and drops me
and my bee. We crash to
the ground with a *squelch*.

As I gasp for breath, I spot Pan.
She stands before the tree in full monk
mode, spiraling her hands before her. She's
the one making the muck elves
cyclone through the air! I had no
idea she could propel actual
people with nothing but

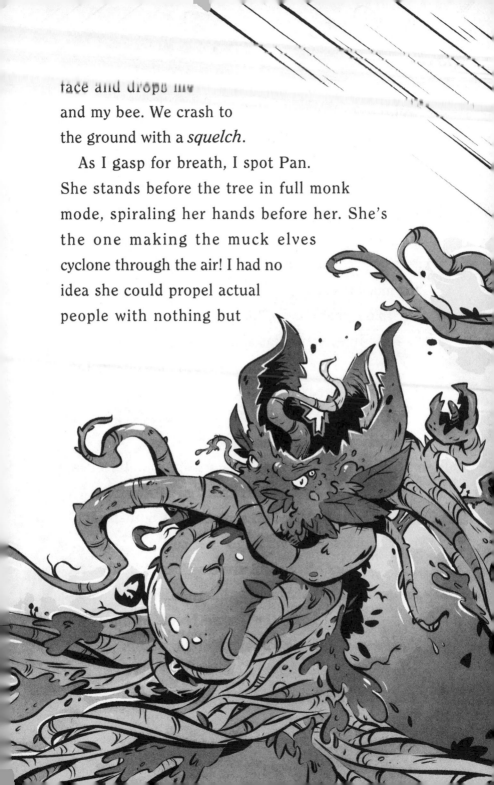

wind power. She has grown more powerful than I realized.

The muck elves fire. SquishRabble roars. But this dance can only go on so long. Peat Blossom and gang are going to run out of arrows any second. And then we're in deep doo-doo.

"Moxie," cries Pan. "Get ready."

"Get ready for what?" Moxie yells over the sound of the muck man's angry roars.

"To do what you do," Pan says.

Pan flings her arms up, sending the muck elves shooting into the air. They effortlessly land on the upper branches of the tree.

Pan concentrates hard and begins to make a slurping sound, like she's sucking through a straw.

SquishRabble shudders. A stream of water gushes from the muck man, flowing straight toward Pan.

She's sucking all the water out of SquishRabble. Leaving him an empty, dry husk.

The muck man shambles toward Pan, eager to reach his precious water. Desperate to get back to his old, squishy self. But he doesn't squelch when he walks now. He crunches. Like brittle branches.

"Now, Moxie!" Pan cries through gritted teeth.

84

When I open my eyes, SquishRabble is just a pile of kindling. And even a baby knows what to do with kindling.

"Flimmity-flamesh," I mutter, sending sparks to the nearest pile. They flare into flame.

SUPERHEROIC ACHIEVEMENT!
Defeat a Muck Man!
(275 Experience Points Awarded)

Pan wobbles, steadying herself against a mucky boulder. The elves drop nimbly to the ground.

"You guys saved me and Bizzy," I cry. Bizzy waggles her bumbly butt in agreement.

"What?" says Peat Blossom.

"Thank you!" I say. "You saved me."

"What?" Peat Blossom says again.

Maybe Peat Blossom took a muck-man bonk to the head. Suddenly she draws her bow. At Pan.

"Whoa! Whoa! Whoa!" says Moxie, holding up her hands.

But Jethro and Boondoggle follow Peat Blossom's lead. They all aim straight for Pan's heart. And open fire.

"The spores!" cries Moxie. "We forgot about the spores!"

The arrows fly fast and true. Straight into the baby muck men that have risen from the sludge behind Pan. The teensy muck men crumble into tiny piles of leaves and vines. TickTock lights them up with a burning twig.

Pan plucks something from her left ear. The muck elves do the same. "Now," she says, "what were you guys blabbering about?"

"That was some impressive wind power, Pan!" crows Moxie.

"Not wind power," says Pan. "I could never lift three elves with just the wind."

"So how did you create an elf-nado?" I ask.

Pan smirks. "Peat Blossom's idea. Remember? She said the muck covering them is just water and earth. I was able to manipulate all the muck on their bodies and send them soaring through the air."

"And you sucked water out of SquishRabble the same way!" TickTock says, grinning. "Good elf brain!"

"But I'm confused about one thing," I say. I turn to Peat Blossom and the muck elves. "You couldn't fight him because of his high-pitched roaring."

"Yep," says Peat Blossom, nodding. "That there screechin' is a menace to elf ears, that's fer sure."

I turn back to Pan. "So how were you able to come back and help us?"

Pan digs out a grayish-green blob from her right ear. "Muck moss," she says.

"Pan's idea," says Peat Blossom. "We've tried every which way of covering up our ears. Never thought about shoving muck moss in 'em. The stuff must be super gloppy for blocking out sound!"

Pan wipes out her ears. "And super disgusting as well."

88

"Hooray!" TickTock jumps up and down. "Muck is saving the day!"

Moxie joins us, something in her hands. "I don't think SquishRabble cared much about treasure," she says. "But I found a few things near the roots of that tree. Must be from some of his former victims." She tosses me a dirty pouch.

I dump out the contents. Several gems and at least fifty gold pieces.

"And this," says Moxie, holding up a dirty piece of cloth. "It's a cloak. It's filthy, but you can tell the material is good."

"Not just good," I say. The ring on my finger tingles and the cloak glows with a familiar blue aura. "That's a magic cloak."

SUPERHEROIC ACHIEVEMENT!
Find a Magic Item!
(200 Experience Points Awarded)

Moxie ties it around her shoulders.

"Gah!" I screech in horror. "Why do you guys always drink the magic potion or put on the magic cloak?! Not all magic is good, you know!"

"Ah," says Moxie sheepishly. "Sorry. But I'm still alive, so it must be okay." She strikes a dashing pose. "How do I look?"

TickTock makes a face. "Very mucky."

Peat Blossom walks over and pats Pan on the back. "A little muck ain't so bad. Is it, princess?"

Pan grins at her. "No, it ain't," she says. "No, it ain't."

CHAPTER THIRTEEN

Meemaw is pleased. She opens her purse and passes out peppermints to all of us for a job well done.

"You are sure, Peat Blossom?" asks Meemaw. "Squish-Rabble is no more?"

"Gone fer good, Meemaw," confirms Peat Blossom. "Shot full of arrows, freshly squeezed, and burned to a crisp." She nods at our group. "These city folk done real good."

"Well, that's a relief, and no mistake!" says Meemaw, rubbing her hands together in satisfaction. "And now it's time for us to hold up our end of the bargain. Because muck elves are true to their word."

Elves come in bearing the rest of our belongings. Pan

bows gratefully as they return her mother's necklace. But Moxie already has what matters most to her: her hammer.

"You are free to go," says Meemaw. "But more than that, you are our friends." She looks at Pan. "If that is something you desire."

Pan steps forward. "It is, Meemaw. Meeting you and your people has given me a lot to think about."

SUPERHEROIC ACHIEVEMENT!
Make Some New Friends!
(300 Experience Points Awarded)

Meemaw's smile lights up the room. "Well, that's all any of us can ask for. Lots to think about." She turns to the rest of us. "It is still your desire to travel to Wetwater?"

Moxie nods. "Yes, ma'am. We have business that takes us there."

"Mm-mm-mm," she hums, shaking her head. "Well, I don't envy you that business. But we can help you on your way. Peat Blossom!"

Boondoggle and Jethro clap their hands excitedly. "Meemaw!" says Boondoggle. "Can we take 'em in the snot rockets?"

Meemaw rolls her eyes. "You boys know I don't like that phrase," she says firmly. Then her eyes sparkle down at Boondoggle. "But yes, Boondoggle. Take 'em in the snot rockets."

I step forward timidly. "Meemaw," I say. "Before we go, I have one more request."

Meemaw chuckles. "Well, request away, child! Be bold!"

I bite my lip nervously. "Can I have another peppermint?"

Meemaw hoots out a laugh. She reaches into her purse. "Honey. You take the whole bag."

We are zipping through Blight Bog Funk at roughly the speed of snot.

SNOT ROCKETS

Pulled by sludge runners.

Hold on to your butt.

TickTock is geeking out over the snot rockets. He's peppering Jethro with suggestions for mechanical gizmos that would make the mud sleds go faster.

As the wind whips through my hair, I realize I've learned a lot during our time in the swamp.

Muck moss works nicely as earplugs.

Pan can tornado-spin people, as long as they're filthy.

But most important . . . I want a snot rocket.

Before long, the city of Wetwater takes over the entire horizon.

I never imagined such a big place could exist.

Peat Blossom pulls up to a patch of firm ground. A road in the distance runs right to the gates of Wetwater.

"This is where we leave y'all," says Peat Blossom.

We unload and face the muck elves. "Thanks, guys," I say. "I never knew many elves, other than Pan. Now I know there are elves that aren't nearly as uptight as she is."

Jethro and Boondoggle guffaw at that. Pan grins and whacks me with her bo staff.

"Farewell, *Panalathalasas*," says Peat Blossom.

"Farewell, *Haselfathselas*," says Pan.

Peat Blossom squints. "What's that jibber-jabber, runt?"

Pan smirks. "That is 'Peat Blossom' in High Elvish."

Peat Blossom shoots Pan a grin. "Hear that, boys?" she calls over her shoulder. "*Haselfathselas!* I'm all fancy!"

The muck elves zip away and are soon lost in the mists of Blight Bog Funk.

CHAPTER FOURTEEN

The city of Wetwater looms before us.

As we approach the massive gates, the guards barely shoot us a look. I was worried we would attract too much attention. After all, we are an odd-looking group. But they barely give us a passing glance.

And then we enter the city. And I see why.

Creatures of every shape and size bustle down the streets before us.

"Is that being an ogre?" asks TickTock, pointing at a massive creature strolling down the street.

"Don't point," says Pan, lowering TickTock's arm. "And yes. That is an ogre."

We retreat under the awning of a nearby tattoo shop, nearly getting stampeded by three turtlemen riding enormous fuzzy beasts.

I turn to Pan. "What do we do?"

Her eyes are as wide as Moxie's shield. But, as usual, her voice is calm. "Kevin said to find his friend."

"That's right," says Moxie. "Magda something. At the Fried Phoenix Inn."

"Hey! You kids looking to get inked?" says a voice. I turn and see a burly guy with an orange goatee, covered in tattoos.

"Inked?" I ask the man, terrified.

"Tattooed!" he clarifies. "Look, bumpkins. I don't got all day. You looking to commemorate your trip to the big city with a little body art, or what? A dragon, maybe? Or a banshee?"

"No thank you," says Pan.

"That's cool. That's cool," says goatee guy. "Then do me a favor?"

"What's that?" I ask.

"GET OFF MY FRONT STOOP!" he roars. "You're driving away legitimate customers with your gawking faces and your country mouse vibe!" He blusters back into the shop.

We walk down the road, ducking around carts being

pulled by weird creatures with horns and trunks and multiple tails. We weave between giant lizardmen and tiny gnomes.

We wander for a couple hours. And then, just when my feet are starting to kill me, Pan spots it.

THE FRIED PHOENIX INN

Best fried phoenix in Wetwater.

Talon-lickin' good!

Magda?

"Look." She points at a large red sign.

"That's the place," I say with a sigh of relief. We push past a band of short birdmen and enter the Fried Phoenix Inn.

Rowdy laughter and gruff talk comes from every corner. Behind a long bar stands a stout lady with purple hair.

MAGDA

Intimidating presence.

Tattoo of a rum barrel.

Booming voice.

"All right," says Pan firmly. "Stay together and let me do the talking."

We squeeze up to the bar, between a surly-looking barbarian and a bugbear who smells like baloney sandwich.

"Is that bee housebroken?" the purple-haired woman demands.

Bizzy looks insulted at the very thought. I pet her comfortingly. "Don't worry," I reassure the woman. "She won't pee on your floors."

"Fair enough," she says. "What'll you lot have?"

"Are you Magda Rumrunner?" Pan asks.

"Owner and proprietor," she growls. "Who be asking?"

"We're friends of the Great and Powerful Kevin," Pan says.

Magda scowls. "That no-good bearded troll? He cost me a lot of money last time he was here!"

Uh-oh. I'm starting to think we've made a terrible mistake. Kevin has fed us bad information before. It almost cost us our lives.

She leans in close. "He's the only one alive who can beat me at jinni stones!" She lets out a hooting laugh, and her face splits into a lopsided smile. "How is old GPK? Has he found himself a nice lady friend to settle down with yet?"

"There is a lady there," pipes in TickTock. "But Kevin is keeping her hidden always. Only hearing her yelling and wailing all the time."

"I can't blame him for that," Pan says, tucking her

necklace into her tunic. "I'd hide her too if I were a forty-year-old man living with my mother."

Magda cringes. "Eek. That's too bad." She pulls out a filthy dishrag and starts wiping down the bar. "So! You guys got a place to stay while you're in Wetwater?"

Pan tucks some stray hair-wispies behind her ear. "We were hoping you could help us with that."

"Well, I'm full up at the moment," says Magda. "However, I always keep some special accommodations open for unexpected friends." She winks. "Or friends of friends."

"It's a broom closet, isn't it?" says Moxie.

Magda winks at her. "You know it, sweetheart. But we'll set up some cots, make it all comfy-cozy for you."

She whistles over her shoulder, and a grizzled troll appears.

"Beezle, go get the VIP room ready for my friends," she says. "And when I say ready, I mean take the outhouse-unclogging stick out of there!" Beezle ambles away.

"Go grab yourselves a table," Magda tells us. "I'll get some grub sent over to you. You're probably tired and hungry."

"Thank you, Magda," says Pan with a small bow.

"Don't mention it, you lot!" she says. "Any friend of that dung-scented, chicken-livered cow of a mage is a friend of mine!"

The inn is packed. But after much scooching, we make it to a tiny empty table in the corner.

"So?" says Moxie, pulling up a stool. "We made it this far. What's the plan?"

Pan fidgets with her hair thoughtfully. "Our strategy is critical now. No improvising. Somehow we must get the location of a bedazzler from the deadly pirate Diremaw the Dread."

"A pirate who nobody but his crew has ever seen," Moxie points out.

"True," says Pan. "Perhaps we can sneak aboard the ship and search his cabin. It is possible that he's recorded the bedazzler's location in a journal."

"Kevin is saying the pirate might pick up supplies," says TickTock.

Pan sighs. "Of course Kevin's information is often unreliable."

"Maybe," concedes the phibling. "But if Diremaw really is getting supplies, maybe we are sneaking into supplies and getting loaded onto his ship."

"Ooh, that's sneaky, TickTock," says Moxie. "I like it. Sneak in. Search for info. Sneak out."

"Well, first we need some info about this Diremaw guy," I say. "We don't even know if he's in the city."

"And above all else," says Pan firmly, "let us avoid any unnecessary trouble."

Suddenly there's a roar from the bar. It's the smelly bugbear.

"Hey!" he yells, lifting a squirming green figure into the air. "That is Grak's coin purse! Thieving goblin scum!"

Grak hurls the goblin across the room. He slams onto one of the tables, knocking liquid all over a brawny dwarf.

"Hey!" the dwarf cries. "Watch where you're throwing goblins!" He grabs his axe, flips the table, and charges the bugbear.

The dwarf's table whacks the barbarian at the bar.

"Hey!" screams the barbarian. "You hit me with table? I hit you with spear!"

The barbarian snatches his spear, knocking drinks from hands all around him.

Suddenly weapons are flying. Tables are smashing. Chairs are hurtling across the room.

We duck under our table.

The goblin who started it all tries to crawl under with us, yanking TickTock out to make room.

"Hey!" cries Moxie. She pushes the goblin back with the tip of her hammer. "You leave my friends alone!"

"Crud on a cracker," I mutter. "I thought we were trying to stay out of trouble."

The armored dwarf sets his axe on the table.

The barbarian drops his spear.

Moxie lowers her hammer.

"THAT'S RIGHT!" says Magda. "NO WEAPONS! FISTS OR FURNITURE! NOTHING ELSE!"

Moxie grabs a chair and smashes it over the goblin's head.

SUPERHEROIC ACHIEVEMENT!

Get into a Bar Fight!

(200 Experience Points Awarded)

We peek out from under the table. Moxie turns to face us, a big grin plastered across her face.

CHAPTER FIFTEEN

The broom closet is not as bad as it sounds.

Sure, there's the vague smell of outhouse-unclogging stick. But TickTock produces some type of propeller-fan contraption from his belt called the Marvelous Spinning Pinwheel of Coolness. It seems to get rid of the outhouse stench. However, it does nothing for the dirty mop smell or the rotten vegetable stink. So it may still need some tinkering.

The next day, we ask Magda about Diremaw the Dread. Her face goes pale when we mention his name. Magda says she doesn't know anything about the comings and goings of pirates.

Smart lady.

But she points us in the direction of the harbor. "Head toward that big blue thing," she says with a sneer. "That's called the ocean. If you find yourself underwater, you went too far."

The harbor hums with activity. Fisherman unload ships. Giant nets hoist huge crates onto boats. Everyone is cursing. And shoving.

"The pirate boat is being named the *Death Knell*," TickTock reminds us.

"Yeah, that's right," says Moxie, nodding. "Maybe we'll see his ship."

We see lots of ships. With lots of weird names.

But no *Death Knell*.

Finally Pan spots something that might help us out:
the harbormaster's office.

"If anyone knows about the *Death Knell*," Pan sur-
mises, "it will be the harbormaster."

A bell dings as we enter the cramped office.
Scrolls and papers and opened books cover
every surface. It looks like a library upchucked
in here.

"What do you want!?" growls a prune of
a man. Every part of this guy is wrinkled.
I find myself with a strong desire to iron
him.

I refrain. "We're looking for information," I say instead.

"Get out of here!" says the prune. "I'm busy!"

Moxie steps up, opens her pouch, and drops five gold coins on the counter. "Still busy?" she asks.

The prune eyeballs the coins. "You triple that and you just might have my attention."

Moxie shells out ten more gold coins from her pouch.

"I'm listening," says the man.

"We're trying to find a specific ship," says Moxie.

"Well, that is information I have." The wrinkled guy puts on a pair of cracked spectacles. "I know every ship that comes and goes from this city." He opens up a ledger. "What's the ship's name?"

"The *Death Knell*," says Pan.

The prune lowers the spectacles from his nose. "What would the likes of you be wanting with a ruthless pirate king?"

Moxie slides five more coins onto the counter. "That would be our business."

The harbormaster looks at the coins. His eyes dart back to us. Uncertain. Finally he slides the coins into his hand.

"Diremaw the Dread has a special reserved parking spot at this harbor," he tells us. "It is one of the courtesies I extend to him." He wets his wrinkled lips. "You'll find it all the way down the harbor," he says, pointing. "Past the North Twin."

"The North Twin?" asks Pan.

"Those giant twin statues that flank the harbor," he growls.

"Got it," I say. "The North Twin."

"Just follow the small path hidden at the statue's base and you'll find Diremaw's Dock."

North
Twin.

South
Twin.

Harbor-
master's
Office.

Somewhere
down here:
Diremaw's
Dock.

"Great," says Moxie. She's already halfway out the door. "Let's go."

"Hold on, me buckos," says the prune. "She ain't there."

"She who?" I ask.

"The *Death Knell*!" he sputters.

"But you just said—"

"I just said that's where she *would be* if she were here!" he says. "But she ain't! Yet."

The prune looks around to make sure nobody is listening. Other than paper mites and dust bunnies, it's just us.

"Diremaw sent a parrot with a message three days ago," he says. "He'll make port tomorrow."

116

"We appreciate the information," says Pan.

"Well, you paid enough," he says. "Only seems right that I give you the whole picture."

"What whole picture?" I ask.

"The parrot had something else," says the harbormaster. "This."

CREW TRYOUTS FOR THE DEATH KNELL

Come join the most notorious pirate to ever sail the 14 seas! Good pay! Medical and dental benefits! Swashbuckling adventure! Apply in person at Diremaw's Dock. First day of autumn, 10 a.m. sharp.

"The first day of autumn?" says Pan. "That's tomorrow."

"This is perfect!" says Moxie with a grin. "Thanks, mister!"

"Be ye careful, me hearties." The prune's whisper stops me cold. "Diremaw the Dread is nobody to trifle with."

Moxie shoots the guy a wink. "Neither are we."

It's the coolest exit line ever. A total lie, of course. We've been nearly trifled to death on several occasions.

CHAPTER SIXTEEN

Moxie leads us down the twisty streets of Wetwater with a bounce in her step.

"This is even better than sneaking aboard with the cargo," she says excitedly. "Nobody has ever seen Diremaw the Dread except his crew! So tomorrow we go to Diremaw's Dock. And we try out for the crew!"

"Crud on a cracker!" I cry. "Hold on a second. If we manage to join his crew, don't you think he'll be a little miffed when we just take off to hunt a bedazzler?"

"Oh, wow," says Moxie. "I didn't think about that."

"I imagine Diremaw doesn't simply let people quit his crew," says Pan.

"So what are we supposed to do?" asks Moxie.

We silently follow Moxie through the crowded streets. Thinking. Puzzling. All of us seeking some solution that doesn't involve a pirate killing us dead.

"What if we do faking our own deaths?" suggests TickTock. "Then the pirate king never is looking for us."

"Ooh, another nice one from TickTock!" says Moxie. "Pirates don't waste time hunting down people that are already dead."

Pan nods thoughtfully. "It is a sound strategy."

"It's great!" Moxie cries enthusiastically. "We join the crew. We get the info. We fake our deaths and make our getaway! Nothing could go wrong!"

There's a nervous feeling creeping into my stomach. It's the feeling I always get when I'm about to fake my own death and wind up getting really dead.

As we duck under a dark archway, I realize we have wandered down a very shady street. The crowds have disappeared. Garbage litters the cobblestones. Rats scurry in the corners.

"I don't remember coming this way before," I tell Moxie. "Where are you taking us?"

"Taking us?" says Moxie, confused. "I'm not taking us anywhere."

"We've been following you," I point out.

"Well, why would you do that?" she asks. "I don't know where I'm going!"

"And that's perfect for us," says a soft voice.

Five ghostlike shapes emerge from the shadows.

One of the hooded figures drops lightly from a drainpipe. She pulls back her hood, revealing a scarlet mask covering her eyes. "How rude of me," she says. "Introductions are in order. My name is Red."

She points to the lurking forms that have surrounded us. "And these are my companions. We are the Skullduggery Crew."

THE SKULLDUGGERY CREW

Cool team name.

Sneaky masks.

Scary weapons.

Total jerks. You'll see.

Red bows politely, pointing a small crossbow at Moxie. "We will be handling your transaction today."

"Transaction?" says Moxie gruffly, squeezing her hammer. "You mean you want to rob us."

"That is a transaction," Red says with a smile. "You give us your possessions. We give you your lives. Everybody gets something."

"One problem," says Moxie, the muscles in her arms tightening. "We're not open for business."

She leaps forward, hammer swinging. The thief fires her crossbow, but Moxie whirls around and the tiny arrow thunks into her shield.

TickTock launches his little arm-mounted web-shooting contraption at one of the thugs. The web wraps around the thief's ankles, and he thumps to the ground.

Pan flings her bola, entangling another goon around the neck.

I begin to call up the words to my Slip 'N Slide spell. But just as I'm about to utter the incantation, something makes me swallow the words back down.

"Moxie," I cry. "Put your weapons down."

"Not this time, Fart!" she cries, swinging ferociously

at Red. "We did that with the muck elves and look where it got us!"

"MOXIE!" yells Pan.

Moxie turns angrily, but what she sees brings her to a stop.

One of Red's crew has a dagger to my throat.

Bizzy buzzes angrily at the sight of me being man-handled. She lashes her stinger.

"Call off the bee," the thief hisses in my ear.

"Down, Bizzy," I choke out. "Sit!"

Bizzy flutters her wings and sits obediently at my feet.

"Very good," says Red. "Now drop your weapons."

Moxie squeezes her hammer so hard that her knuckles turn white. For a long moment I think she's going to keep fighting.

But then the hammer drops to the cobbles with a ringing *thud*.

Red's crossbow is reloaded and pointing at Moxie. "Sorlag, be a dear," she says. "Gather their valuables, if you would."

The stocky thief steps forward and hefts Moxie's hammer appreciatively.

"No!" Moxie says through gritted teeth. She's trying hard to hold it together.

"Don't worry," says the robber with a wicked smile. "I'm going to give this fine hammer a very good home."

He grabs Moxie's shield. Cuts the coin pouch from her waist. All five hundred gold pieces that Kevin paid us, plus her magical animal figures. Gone.

The thieves snatch Pan's bo staff, the sweet one she got at the lamia's lair. They aren't interested in her other simple weapons, but they cut the strings on her bola.

"Let's not forget this," my captor hisses in my ear. I can smell his bitter breath as he reaches for my staff.

ZAP!

With a blinding flash of green he pulls away his hand painfully.

"You idiot," says Red. "You can't take a mage's staff. They are magically linked to their rightful owners."

The thief eyeballs my spellbook, my ring, and my dagger, but then thinks better of it. He slides his blade from my throat and walks back to his boss, rubbing his sore hand.

The thieves grabs us roughly, shoving our faces against the dirty brick wall.

This is it. This is how we die. In a filthy alley, with a dagger to the back.

I close my eyes, waiting for them to finish us.

But it never comes.

A moment passes. Five. Ten.

We slowly turn around.

The Skullduggery Crew is gone. Along with most of our possessions.

"I hate this city," Moxie says.

CHAPTER SEVENTEEN

Moxie is completely shattered by our encounter with the thieves.

Back in our broom closet, Pan uses her monkly might to heal our scrapes and bruises. But she has no power to heal whatever is going on inside of Moxie.

"Don't worry," I say, trying to encourage her. "Yes, that was a lot of gold that they stole. But when we get done with this quest, Kevin will pay us plenty more!"

"I don't care about the gold," she mutters.

"I know it was humiliating," murmurs Pan. "Being robbed like that."

"I don't care about that!" growls Moxie.

"Then what is being wrong, Hammer-girl?" asks TickTock.

Her anger bubbles to the surface. Her face clenches, turning red. Finally the dam breaks and tears stream down her face. "My hammer!" she cries. "They took Master Redmane's hammer!"

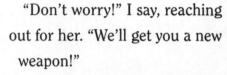

"Don't worry!" I say, reaching out for her. "We'll get you a new weapon!"

"Yes," cries TickTock. "Tick-Tock is keeping a little gold here in our room! We can be buying you a cool sword or a mace!"

"You don't understand!" Moxie cries. "That was Master Redmane's hammer! Ever since I was a little girl, he had that hammer on his belt. It was the one thing I had left of him, and it was everything to me. EVERYTHING! And now it's gone!"

"But . . ." I start. But there's nothing good to say.

Moxie curls into a ball on her cot. "Please. Just leave me alone."

The broom closet is thick with discouragement and defeat.

It also smells like poop. Which is probably because the outhouse-unclogging stick is back.

"Well," says Pan softly. "Our encounter with the Skullduggery Crew was unfortunate, but it did give me an idea." She pulls a dishrag off a shelf.

"What is elf-girl's idea?" asks TickTock.

Pan wraps the cloth around her eyes like a blindfold. Or a mask. "I don't think we should let this pirate know who we really are," she says. "We plan to betray him, after all. In case things go awry, we should hide our true identities."

"Sneaky," I tell her. "Wear masks."

"It would be prudent," says Pan.

It's been a terrible day and it's late. We roll over and try to sleep. I lay there patting Bizzy, but all I can think of is the feeling of that cruel dagger at my throat.

And Moxie's face as she dropped her war hammer to save my life.

Helplessness and frustration overwhelm me. What could I have done differently? I guess I could have cast Gas Attack on the thief with the dagger. But the others would have just finished us off.

If I had known some truly powerful magic, those thieves would have been at my mercy. My brain keeps going back to that Mind Control spell. If I knew that spell, I could have made those thieves do whatever I wanted. And Moxie would still have her hammer.

Grabbing my spellbook, I slip out of our broom closet and into the bar. It's quiet at this late hour, but a few logs still burn in the phoenix-shaped fireplace.

I open my spellbook on a table and flip to the back.

Once again, Master Elmore's voice gripes at me. *Don't be a ninny! You're not ready for this kind of magic!*

I don't care. I swear to myself that the next time I'm in a dangerous situation, I will be ready to unleash real power. A little niggling part of me wonders if it's okay to control people's minds. But I brush away the thought. After all, anyone I'm gonna cast it on is vile and despicable and totally deserves it.

And with that thought, I begin to memorize Mind Control.

CHAPTER EIGHTEEN

The next day, we pool together our remaining possessions.

I lucked out. My staff, my spellbook, my scrolls—they didn't take any of it.

Luckily, Pan's favorite necklace was tucked under her tunic, so the thieves never found it. Even so, she lost all her gold and weapons. But that girl could make a weapon out of a pine cone, so she's not too worried.

It's Moxie that came out the worst. No gold. No shield. No hammer. And no fight left in her.

Pan says that our plan has no place for a loudly buzzing insect the size of a baby elephant. I don't like it, but

I finally give in. Magda gruffly insists she isn't running a bee-sitting service, but after slipping her a couple gold coins, she agrees to keep an eye on Bizzy until we get back. If we get back.

So, with a tearful farewell to Bizzy, we take Tick-Tock's remaining cash and go shopping.

We manage to find the phibling a new dagger and Moxie a worn secondhand sword. She doesn't say a word as she slides it into her belt.

And we buy four snazzy silk masks. We look super sinister.

Super sinister.

Just like the Skullduggery Crew.

Stupid Skullduggery Crew.

Told you they were jerks.

As we stand outside the shop, Pan gives a little sermon against improvising. "Please just remember the plan," she reminds us. "Join the crew. Get the location of the bedazzler from Diremaw. Fake our deaths and disappear."

We all nod grimly.

"Look, guys. I know we had a rough day yesterday," I tell them. "But we've got a big job to do today. And we're probably going to die. But there's nobody I'd rather die with!"

Pan rolls her eyes. "Worst pep talk ever."

Moxie manages a small smile. Her eyes are still sad. But I'll take it.

We head toward the harbor, paying careful attention this time. No more getting lost. And robbed. And emotionally scarred.

The shadow from the enormous statue falls across us as we enter the harbor. The North Twin.

"Look," says TickTock, pointing.

Near the base, tucked behind some scrub, is a small, planked path.

It meanders into a small, secluded cove. And there, parked in its reserved spot, is a ruthless-looking ship.

Crud on a cracker. That is one pirate-y ship. I expected that. What I didn't expect is the line of people. Apparently word has gotten around that Diremaw the Dread is holding tryouts.

We join the crowd. And that's when I spot a familiar lumbering form at the end of the line.

"Bucket?" I gasp.

A runty ogre turns around at the sound of his name.

Bucket stares at us with concern. "How you know Bucket?"

The masks! I lift my mask so he can see my face. "It's us! Remember?"

A look of realization washes across his face. "Little magic man!" he says. "It you!"

Pirate-y figurehead: an enormous bell made of bones.

Pirate-y black hull.

BUCKET

Runty ogre.

Saved our necks once.

All-around good guy.

Clean loincloth, by ogre standards.

"Hello, Bucket," says Pan, raising her mask slightly in greeting.

"Elf-girl!" says Bucket in recognition. "You naughty! Put Bucket to sleep last time I see you!"

"I did," Pan admits.

"Frog boy! Hi, orange-hair girl!"

"Hey, Bucket," says Moxie. "What are you doing here?"

"After Bucket wake up, other ogres never come back," he says. He pulls out a little sketch pad and opens it up. "Look! Bucket draw'd a comic about his adventures!"

He smiles. "Now Bucket here! And seeing old friends!"

Aw. I don't know if I'd call us friends or not. Still. You gotta love his attitude.

"You drew that?" asks Moxie. "That's really good."

"Thanks, orange-hair girl!" The little ogre is all smiles.

"ALL RIGHT, YOU LUBBERS! LISTEN UP!" We turn. A tiny gnome looms over us from the ship. "I BE FIRST MATE TIDEPOOL!" she roars. "AND THESE . . . are the *Death Knell* crew tryouts!"

The crowd cheers.

"We've only got five open spots," Tidepool yells.

FIRST MATE
TIDEPOOL

Tiny but
terrifying.

"FIVE! So break yourselves up into teams of five. Then come on board!"

"But friends!" TickTock hisses. "We are being only four!"

Pan turns to the ogre. "Bucket, would you care to join our team?"

A big goofy grin washes across his face. "Bucket like that! Bucket never on a team! Only on potty bucket duty."

Potty. Doody. Heh.

"One thing though," whispers Bucket. "Where you get cool masks? Bucket wants one too."

CHAPTER NINETEEN

We're the only team wearing masks. I think it gives us that extra something special.

The pirate crew gathers around to watch the fun. They snicker behind their hands and boo us.

And that's when a door slams open. A barrel-chested dwarf swaggers out. His wild red beard glistens with sea spray and his hands clutch a terra-cotta pot. "I've arrived!" he cries. "We can begin!"

"Perhaps this is Diremaw the Dread," says Pan, eyeballing the dwarf.

The other pirates howl with laughter.

"Hear that?" shouts a one-armed pirate. "She thinks Cookie is Diremaw the Dread!"

"Aye, Captain Cookie!" cries one with an eye patch. "Man the frying pan!"

"What do you say to that, Cookie?" yells a third pirate, slapping the dwarf on the back.

Cookie hugs the flowerpot closer. "I says that Diremaw the Dread is captain of this ship!" he growls. "And I be captain of me kitchen!"

"Um . . ." I point at the pot. A small red plant sprouts from the dirt. "What's with the flowerpot?"

The dwarf guffaws loudly. "Hear that, lads? The lubber thinks I'm holding a flowerpot!" He holds up the pot proudly. "This here is no flower," he says. "It's a devilfern. It's the most ruthless, savage, cold-blooded potted plant ever to sail the fourteen seas! And his name . . . is Ferny."

COOKIE AND FERNY

Both . . . ruthless pirates.

Both . . . possibly one potato short of a stew.

"He loves that plant more than life!" groans one of the pirates. "Waters it every day at six o'clock! No matter what! Nothing comes before that plant!"

The plant suddenly points a leaf at Pan. "Who let this elf in here?" it squawks. "She looks like a goblin with too much hair gel!"

The dwarf bellows with laughter. "HA! I told you he was ruthless!"

"ALL RIGHT!" roars First Mate Tidepool. "LISTEN UP, YOU MANGY DOGS!"

"Belay that, Ms. Tidepool!" interrupts Cookie. "I need one of these newbies to help me in the kitchen! I've got potatoes to peel and the captain's feast to prepare! Plus Ferny will need watering won't you, Ferny? Won't you?"

The devilfern squawks loudly. "Six o'clock! Don't be late!"

"Who's a smart devilfern?" coos Cookie. "Who knows what time he gets watered?"

"Ferny does! Ferny does!" yells the plant.

Tidepool scans the line of new recruits before her eyes fall on our little group.

"Dwarf!" she stabs a finger at Moxie. "Judging by that

sorry sword on your belt, you'll be no good in a fight. Perhaps you can put it to better use in the kitchen!"

Moxie looks at us anxiously.

"Let's go, lass," Cookie cries to Moxie. "You've been assigned to me! And those potatoes aren't going to peel themselves!" The dwarf opens the door and heads belowdecks. And Moxie slowly follows.

"Moxie!" I cry.

"Hammer-girl!" cries TickTock.

I wait for her to put up a fight. But the fight has gone out of her.

Moxie holds up her hand in some silent signal. Like she's saying it'll be okay. She shoots us a sad smile and the door slams to a close behind her.

We've been separated. This is not part of the plan. I barely have time to wrap my brain around it. Because First Mate Tidepool is ushering us down some steps.

"THIS WAY, YOU SCURVY LUBBERS!" she cries. "And be quick about it!"

We follow her into the belly of the ship. Rats skitter in the shadows. The whole place smells dank, like a swamp and a bog had a baby and that baby ate a whole pot of fish heads and did diarrhea in its diaper. Which is what you get when you feed a baby fish heads. Honestly, who does that?

First Mate Tidepool stands before us in the swinging lantern light.

"All right, recruits!" she yells. "We have three teams. What are your team names?"

"We're the Fluffy Unicorn Gang!" croaks a huge half-orc.

THE FLUFFY UNICORN GANG

Human Barbarian. The muscle.

Half-Orc Warrior. The leader.

Gnoll Stalker. The crazy one.

Dwarf Pyromancer. The spitfire.

Fuzznik Archer. The fuzzy silent type.

"We be the Bad-Breath Bandits!" says a hairy guy who looks like a weasel.

THE BAD-BREATH BANDITS

Weasel Guy. Horrible breath.

Troll Cutthroat. Scary nose hairs.

Human Scoundrel. Dandruff problems.

Tuskin Vagabond. Eye boogers for days.

Goblin Sneakthief. Smells like armpit.

Terrible hygiene seems to be a running theme.

Tidepool looks at us. "What about you lot?"

Pan doesn't hesitate. "We are the Skullduggery Crew."

"Ooh," says Tidepool. "Cool name."

The gnome points to a bunch of hammocks. "Bad-Breath Bandits! You'll bunk here for the duration of the tryouts. Fluffy Unicorn Gang! You're here! And Skull-duggery Crew! That puts you over there."

"Bunking?" asks the weasel guy. "How long are these tryouts going to take?"

"Well, that's up to you!" Tidepool roars out a laugh. "You'll be given a complex challenge. The team that performs the challenge best, wins!"

The half-orc raises her hand. "What happens if we don't win?" she asks.

"Ah," says Tidepool with a smile. "You'll all get gold ribbons for trying your best."

"Really?" says Weasel, smiling.

"NO, NOT REALLY!" the first mate roars. "You're going to receive this challenge from Captain Diremaw the Dread personally! And, aside from his crew, NOBODY has ever seen Diremaw the Dread and lived to tell the tale."

She picks something from her teeth and flicks it away. "Which means the team that wins will join the crew! And the teams that don't . . ."

We all look at one another. Whispers of confusion move among us.

Tidepool snickers. "Well, like I said. Nobody meets Diremaw the Dread and lives to tell the tale."

Weasel looks like he might wet himself. "I—I—I think I changed my mind," he stutters. "I don't think I want to try out after all."

Tidepool nods. "Of course, I understand." She looks around. "If anyone else feels that way, there're no hard feelings. I'll just take you up to the main deck and you can get off the ship."

The peg-legged gnome leads us up the stairs.

I look nervously at Pan and TickTock. "A challenge to the death?" I whisper to them. "Are you kidding me?"

"That is an unexpected development," Pan says softly.

"This was a terrible idea," I hiss.

Pan and TickTock nod in agreement.

We emerge into the sunlight, and Tidepool gestures grandly toward the dock. "Any that wish to leave may certainly part company with us at this time. And good luck to you."

I turn to Pan. "I'll go find Moxie. And then we'll get out of here."

"No need, Fart-boy," says TickTock. "Looky-look."

There is no dock.

There is no land.

"Oh, I forgot to mention," says Tidepool with a smile. "We set sail a wee bit ago. Wetwater is a five-mile swim thataway."

CHAPTER TWENTY

We are prisoners on a pirate ship.

That pirate ship is led by the most fearsome pirate captain ever to sail the fourteen seas.

And that pirate captain never leaves prisoners alive.

I may puke.

I wonder if Kevin would be able to tell the difference if I brought him back a bag of my own barf instead of bedazzler barf. Probably. He seems to know way too much about barf.

Stupid Kevin.

In the meantime, Tidepool has put us to work swabbing the deck. Which is just a fancy word for scrubbing fish guts off the floor. The pirates stand around jeering and throwing things at us.

Stupid pirates.

Suddenly Tidepool claps her hands together. "All right, lads and lassies! Eyes on!" she roars.

The jeers have stopped. Every pirate stands at attention before the tiny first mate.

"We make for the Hag's Hangnail!" she calls. "Lower the yard! Furl sail! Sheet home! And full speed ahead!"

"Aye, Ms. Tidepool!" the pirates yell in one voice. And they sprint into action.

A few seconds ago these smelly, rowdy pirates were picking their noses and flicking boogers at us. Now they are a unified orchestra of movement. Sailors scuttle up ropes in unison. Sails unfurl and catch the wind in perfect harmony. It is a concert of movement. A symphony of productivity.

"Wow," Pan whispers in awe. "That's impressive."

"Back to your swabbing, recruits!" Tidepool calls to us. Pan continues scrubbing. But she can't pull her eyes away from the flurry of coordination around us.

Hours later, we lie in our hammocks. The other teams are as exhausted as we are from all the swabbing. I hear nothing but snores from the Bad-Breath Bandits and the Fluffy Unicorn Gang.

Bucket makes little *scratch-scratch* marks in his sketch pad. What could this ogre be doing? I crane my neck to look.

He's drawing Moxie.

"That's incredible," I tell him.

The ogre blushes. "Really think so?" he asks. "Bucket always like to draw. Bucket wish ogres could get paid to make pictures. But ogres only get paid to be mean. And to empty potty buckets."

He sighs and closes his pad. "Maybe being a pirate be different for Bucket."

"Don't count on it," I say. "These pirates are plenty mean. And they all smell like potty buckets."

"Perhaps," says Pan. "But you have to admire the sense of order. It is quite soothing."

149

I chuckle. "You're defending them? They're filthy. They stink. And they made you scrub fish guts all day."

"True," she says. "But there is a hierarchy of command on this ship that leads to efficiency. It is a balm to my road-weary soul."

I'm not sure what this elf is jabbering about. "You're a balm," I say. "A weird one."

"The adventuring life has proven to be quite chaotic," she confesses. "I'm simply noting that the *Death Knell* is truly a well-oiled machine. That sense of reassuring order appeals to me greatly."

TickTock nods approvingly. "TickTock does appreciate a well-oiled machine."

I shake my head. "Regardless, we've got bigger problems. How are we going to win this challenge?"

"And without orange-hair girl?" Bucket adds.

"Yeah," I agree. "Without Moxie!"

"You're right," says Pan. "We need her. But we cannot adequately form a new plan until we know what the challenge is." She shrugs grimly. "You know how I hate improvising. But I think we must do as Moxie so often suggests: Let's burn that bridge when we get to it."

I'm starting to hate that saying.

The three of them roll over, and soon I hear soft snores. But I've got a knot in my gut about what tomorrow may hold. Whatever it is, I want to be ready.

I pull out my spellbook and plunk it onto my hammock. It flops open to a first-level spell.

Easy first-level spell.
No verbal components. Just
simple hand gestures.
Makes anyone you touch
obey a simple suggestion.

Suggestion must
be no longer than
three words.

Huh. It's a little like Mind Control. A beginner version. A baby version.

It's so easy. Snap my fingers. Twirl my wrists. Touch my enemy. Give a command. I'm not sure why I haven't learned it before.

Because it's useless, that's why. What good is a three-word suggestion?

I flip to the Mind Control spell.

I try to focus on the confusing and complex symbols. I mumble them, trying to get my tongue to pronounce them correctly. I think I'm making progress, but it's slow, wearisome work.

I drift off to sleep. I dream of magic. I dream of power. I dream of being able to make people do exactly what I want them to do.

CHAPTER TWENTY-ONE

I wake up to clanging bells.

Shouts come from the upper decks. "Hangnail ho!"

And suddenly my stomach knots up again. Because
I've only been around all this boat lingo for a day. But
it's long enough for me to guess what that means.

It's time for our challenge.

"I want all three teams up on the main deck in ten minutes!" yells Tidepool, blustering back upstairs. "It's time to meet the captain!"

"Bucket so excited!" the little ogre says. "Bucket never been part of a team before!"

"Well, you'll get your chance today," says Pan encouragingly.

"Have you ever died before, Bucket?" I ask.

"No. Bucket never died before."

I smile grimly. "Well, you may get your chance for that today, too."

"OVER HERE, YOU LUBBERS!" roars Tidepool. Her arms rest on the hilt of her barnacle-encrusted sword.

The gnome grandly gestures to an iron-plated door behind her.

"Behind this door is the dread of the high seas. The scourge of the Fourteen Realms. The bane of the lily-livered and the mackerel-hearted. These are the personal quarters of Captain Diremaw himself!"

I feel a chill run up and down my spine that has nothing to do with the crisp morning breeze.

"Captain Diremaw has requested your presence." Tidepool pulls the door wide. "Beware, all ye who enter here," she says ominously. Then she busts out laughing. "I'm just joking! Come on in!"

I take one more glance at the bright blue sky. And then we follow the gnome into the darkened chamber.

Cookie fusses around a small table, his pet devilfern at his side.

The plant points a leaf at me as soon as it spots me. "Ready your pacifiers! Diaper baby off the port bow!"

Gosh, I hate that plant.

"Pipe down, Ferny," hisses the dwarf. Then I spot Moxie. Her armor is gone, replaced by a black apron. The hand-me-down sword on her belt has been joined by an assortment of kitchen utensils. That mucky cape still covers her shoulders, which is probably a serious health code violation. She's helping Cookie set up an elaborate snack tray. But not for us.

For Diremaw the Dread.

"So!" A deep voice rolls from the far end of the cabin. "Are these our new recruits, then, Ms. Tidepool?"

"Aye, Captain," says Tidepool. "That they are."

I look to the voice. Behind a large desk sits a high-backed chair of red leather. It faces away from us. But there's no doubt who sits there.

"I always look forward to meeting potential crew-mates," comes the voice. "My crew is like my family. And families share secrets."

In this strange moment, I think of Kevin. He said we

would find the answers we seek with this man. I hope, for all our sakes, he knows what he's talking about.

"You will be treated like family today," says the voice. "You will learn a terrible secret. The identity of Diremaw the Dread. Unfortunately, only five of you will be around long enough to appreciate such a secret."

The chair spins slowly around. And there he sits. Diremaw the Dread.

I look at Pan. And gulp.

Stupid Kevin.

Once more, he has given us some serious misinformation. "There's one man alive who knows the whereabouts of a living, breathing bedazzler," he had told us. "And that's Diremaw the Dread."

But he was wrong.

Diremaw the Dread doesn't know the location of a bedazzler.

Diremaw the Dread IS a bedazzler.

CHAPTER TWENTY-TWO

The bedazzler scrutinizes each of us in turn with that huge bloodshot eye.

"You are surrounded by the riches and rewards that await you as part of my crew," he says, nodding to piles of golden treasure that litter the room. He floats toward us, a huge repulsive globe of evil.

But he's being super polite. Which is nice.

"Gold," he continues. "Jewels. Rich tapestries. Exotic treasures from faraway places."

"What are these?" asks Weasel, pointing to the glass-domed objects.

"YOU SHUT YOUR MOUTH!" roars Tidepool, smacking him. "You don't speak unless your captain tells you to speak."

"Tidepool, please," says the bedazzler. "It's all right. These are our guests." The enormous orb turns its eye on the weasel guy. "I see you have an appreciation for the rare and unusual, my friend."

Diremaw floats over to the glass dome. "I am a collector, you see. And I confess that I have an appetite. Isn't that right, Cookie?"

"Right ye are, Captain," says Cookie. Moxie stands next to the red-bearded dwarf, eyes wide.

"I love to have my taste buds tantalized!" says the bedazzler. "So I have collected some of

the most rare and savory treats from all over the Fourteen Realms!" The great eye peers into the glass dome. Inside are what seem to be . . . breadsticks.

"Behold!" says Diremaw.

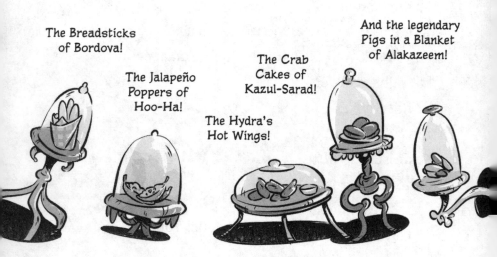

The Breadsticks of Bordova!

The Jalapeño Poppers of Hoo-Ha!

The Crab Cakes of Kazul-Sarad!

The Hydra's Hot Wings!

And the legendary Pigs in a Blanket of Alakazeem!

The creature quivers with joy. "I find these rare delicacies. I gobble down half. And I petrify the other half for my collection!"

He floats to an empty glass dome. "But alas . . . one delicacy has evaded me."

To dream
the impossible
dream...

He perks up. "Until today! That's
where you come in!" A deep growl
fills the room. It's coming from . . . the bedazzler's . . . stomach?

"Please do excuse me!" he says, flushing. "All this
excitement has given me the munchies!" The bedazzler
drifts to the snack table. "Ah, Cookie! You've brought
me nachos!"

"Of course, Captain," says the dwarf. "I knows how
meeting new people makes ye hungry."

"You think of everything!" The creature's enormous
mouth opens wide to devour the tableful of nachos that
Cookie and Moxie have prepared.

But then the bedazzler stops.

He sniffs.

161

And he turns to the dwarf. "Cookie?"

"Yes, Captain?"

"Do I smell . . . *cilantro*?"

CILANTRO

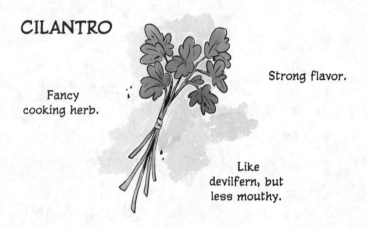

Fancy cooking herb.

Strong flavor.

Like devilfern, but less mouthy.

"Cilantro!" squawks Ferny.

"Yes indeed, Captain!" says Cookie proudly. "It's in the guacamole. It really gives it some zing. I think you'll love it!"

"But I won't, Cookie," says Diremaw calmly.

"You won't?" The dwarf suddenly looks nervous.

"No," says Diremaw. "And do you know why? Because I HATE CILANTRO! JUST THE THOUGHT OF CILANTRO IS ENOUGH TO MAKE ME GAG!!!"

The entire room cowers at the wrath of the terrible beast before us. The tooth bared, the eye wide, the gemstones sparkling with menace. I would say it's the stuff of nightmares. But I don't have enough imagination to dream up something this horrific.

"DO YOU WANT ME TO GAG, COOKIE?" Diremaw roars.

Cookie's ruddy complexion has gone ghostly white. "No, Captain," he says, groveling pitifully. "I . . . I . . . I forgot!"

One of Diremaw's gemstones shoots a little lightning bolt at Cookie's butt. The dwarf yowls in pain.

"That was a warning shot, Cookie," says the bedazzler. "I like you. You're a good cook. But NO CILANTRO!"

"Yes, Captain!" Cookie cries.

"Next time you get the disintegration ray," says Diremaw calmly.

"Beware the disintegration ray!" croaks Ferny.

"I would expect nothing less, Captain!" Cookie snatches up the nachos in one hand, grabs Ferny's pot in the other, and hurries out, leaving Moxie with a spoon in her hand and a terrified expression on her face.

The bedazzler turns to us. "See? One big happy family!"

Gulp. And I thought I had family issues.

The bedazzler floats back to his chair and takes a seat. "Well!" he says. "I suppose you're ready to hear about your challenge."

We nod nervously.

"Your challenge is a treasure hunt!" he says grandly. "I'm looking to add the final missing piece to my delicious collection. This special snacky delight is known as the Kraken's Flatbread!"

The Kraken's Flatbread. An ominous name, to be sure. A chill of dread fills my heart at the sound of it.

But the bedazzler is giddy with excitement. "I can't wait!" he says, bouncing up and down in his chair. "I can't wait to taste its nommy-liciousness! NUM! NUMMY! NUM! NUM!"

Diremaw rises from his seat and floats to the door. "Follow me, my friends," he says, leading us out. "To riches! To treasures! To the Kraken's Flatbread!"

Everyone follows Diremaw and Tidepool out to the main deck. But we hang back.

"Hello, Moxie," Pan whispers.

"Hey, guys," says Moxie. "This challenge sounds intense."

"Yes, it does," says Pan. "That's why you need to come with us."

"I don't know, guys," she says uncertainly. "They've assigned me to the kitchen."

"We need a warrior with us," Pan points out.

"Yeah, Hammer-girl—" TickTock begins.

She cuts him off. "Don't call me that. I don't have a hammer anymore. I'm not Hammer-girl," she says. She pulls out her sad secondhand sword. "Maybe I'm right where I belong. Peeling potatoes."

"Crud on a cracker!" I say fiercely. "I don't care what we call you! Moxie! Hammer-girl! Nacho McCheesy! Whoever you are, we need you."

"Fart, I—"

"You are smart!" I cut her off.

"That's very true," says Pan. "You know more about monsters than anyone alive."

"You face every challenge with a smile!" I tell her.

"Yes!" agrees TickTock. "Hammer-girl always smiles! Even when there is danger!"

"Not only that!" chimes in Bucket. "But also got nice orange hair."

Not really helpful. But at least encouraging.

"But more important," I continue, "you are our friend. And we need you."

She looks at each of us.

"MOXIE!" It's Cookie, calling from the deck. "GET OUT HERE, LASS!"

"I better go," Moxie says, her eyes darting toward the door. "If the kitchen doesn't get cleaned right after breakfast, Master Redmane gets very cranky."

"Master Redmane?" asks Pan. "You mean Cookie."

Moxie's face goes bright red. Her eyes slide to the floor. "See? I'm no good to you like this," she says sadly. "Not without my hammer."

"Moxie Battleborne," I say, lifting her chin. "You are more than just a hammer."

She looks at me sadly. She sighs. And she shakes her head.

"Sorry, guys," she says. "I gotta go."

She grabs her spoon. Her tongs. Her meat tenderizer. And she dashes out the door.

Leaving us with way less moxie than we need. Way less.

CHAPTER TWENTY-THREE

We are heavyhearted as we gather on the deck around Diremaw the Dread.

A huge jagged rock juts from the waves not far away, a dark cave gaping ominously at its base. "That bit of stone there," he says, nodding at the rock. "It is known as the Hag's Hangnail."

The crew gathers around to watch the show. Moxie stands among them, staring blankly ahead.

"Your hunt for the Kraken's Flatbread begins here," Diremaw says.

The rock is littered with wood and debris. The remains of a shipwreck. Something bad happened here.

"The tale is a sad one," the captain says. "Full of woe. And baking."

THE TALE OF JULIETTE KIDD

(AS TOLD BY DIREMAW THE DREAD)

SOME YEARS AGO, THERE LIVED THE GREATEST CHEF IN THE FOURTEEN REALMS. HER NAME WAS JULIETTE KIDD. SHE LOVED THE SEA AND BUILT A MAGNIFICENT FLOATING KITCHEN,

...A GRAND SHIP CALLED THE TANGERINE.

VERY SKILLED IN THE MAGICAL ARTS, SHE EARNED THE NAME THE "MAGICAN OF THE KITCHEN."

JULIETTE KIDD WAS SAILING THESE WATERS. SHE HAD JUST MADE HER GREATEST CREATION: A CRUSTY, CRISPY FLATBREAD THE LIKE OF WHICH HAS NEVER BEEN SEEN IN THIS WORLD.

BUT JUST AS SHE WAS ABOUT TO SERVE IT TO HER CREW, HER SHIP WAS ATTACKED BY A KRAKEN.

THE KRAKEN PULLED JULIETTE KIDD'S SHIP AGAINST THE ROCKS OF THE HAG'S HANGNAIL, INTO YONDER CAVE. NEVER TO BE SEEN AGAIN.

THE MAGICIAN OF THE KITCHEN WAS NO MORE.

SHE COULD HAVE SAVED HERSELF WITH HER MAGIC.

SHE COULD HAVE SAVED HER CREW.

BUT SHE DIDN'T. SHE MADE THE MORE NOBLE CHOICE.

SHE SAVED THE FLATBREAD...

PRESERVING IT IN A SPELL OF PROTECTION JUST AS HER SHIP WAS PULLED INTO THE KRAKEN'S LAIR.

AND THERE IT WAITS, JUST AS FRESH AND DELICIOUS AS THE DAY IT WAS MADE. WAITING FOR THE BRAVE SOULS WITH THE COURAGE TO PLUCK IT FROM THE BRINE.

DRAWN BY BUCKET

The dreamy look leaves Diremaw's eye. He blinks back a tear and looks out upon the gaping opening. The water is much lower than it was before. Almost the entire entrance is showing.

"Inside yonder cave lies the kraken's lair," Tidepool says ominously. "As you can see, the tide is low. Only during low tide can you get in." She cracks her neck noisily. "Or out."

"Within the kraken's lair lies the wreckage of the *Tangerine*," says Diremaw. "And Juliette Kidd's lost flatbread." The bedazzler turns his piercing gaze back upon us. "Bring the Kraken's Flatbread to me."

"How long does low tide last?" asks Pan.

"Good question!" Tidepool looks at the position of the sun. "I'd say you have about five hours until that cave is filled with water once again. You don't want to be inside when that happens."

Weasel has turned green. It's not a good color on him. He looks over at the other Bad-Breath Bandits nervously. "But I'm not a good swimmer!"

Diremaw lets out a belly laugh. "Then I suggest you hold on to somebody who is!"

The crew snickers. Some look amused. Some look terrified. But they all look like they're glad they aren't us.

The bedazzler smiles broadly. "The first team to return with the flatbread will be welcomed into the *Death Knell*'s family! The other teams . . ." He trails off and turns to his first mate.

Tidepool shrugs.

It's a shrug that means if we don't have the flatbread, we should just stay in the cave. Because we're doomed either way. I hate that shrug.

"Best get moving," says Tidepool. "High tide is in less than five hours. On your marks. Get set. Go."

Nobody moves.

The Bad-Breath Bandits looks like they might hurl. The Fluffy Unicorn Gang seems to have a sudden interest in their fingernails.

I hesitate on the ship's edge. "I'm not sure I can do this," I whisper.

"Don't worry," says Pan. She puts her arm around my shoulders. She gives me a reassuring smile.

And she pushes me in.

I seem to fall in slow motion. I hit the water with a splash. Bubbles, brine, and blue surround me.

And then something grabs my leg.

CHAPTER TWENTY-FOUR

Gurblins are pulling me under.

I start to cast Magic Missile at the slimy sucker that's gripping my leg, but I get a mouthful of salt water for my trouble. Instead I give it a swift poke in the face with my staff. It lets go of my leg, and I surge to the surface. But as soon as I gasp for air, two more tug me under again.

Through the bubbles, I see Pan has her hands full with gurblins of her own. And Bucket. I can't see Tick-Tock through the foam.

There's no nice way to say it. We're in deep dookie.

I jab with my staff again. But these fish goblins aren't even trying to fight me. They know if they drag me down, the water will take care of things for them.

GURBLIN

Water goblin.

Seaweed armpit hair for extra nastiness.

Trident for painful stabbing.

Webbed feet for speedy swimming.

I manage to shake loose the gurblins and jet toward daylight. I catch a glimpse of Pan and TickTock fighting off a couple others. My head breaks the surface, and I suck in precious oxygen.

"Pew-pew-patchoo!" I shout quickly, aiming a Magic Missile at the gurblins below me. Bolts of energy nail the one playing snatch-and-grab with my leg.

SIZZLE!

But two more replace it. My lungs swallow one

173

more mouthful of air, and then I'm yanked under again.

I take one last look at the sunlight above me before I am dragged to the depths forever.

Suddenly the slimy hands release me. I fight my flowing robes and swim again for the surface.

As my head breaks the waves, I spot a familiar mane of reddish-orange hair.

Moxie.

Clever girl. The gurblins were dragging us under so we couldn't breathe. Moxie's holding *them* above water so they can't breathe.

I fire off a couple more bolts of energy at the gurb-

lins in her grip. And then I turn and swim for the only solid land in sight.

THE HAG'S HANGNAIL

A cave entrance.

Partly covered in water.

I've never seen a hag's hangnail, but apparently it looks like this.

I'm not a strong swimmer. But Moxie comes to my rescue again and drags me to the rock before exhaustion overtakes me.

I haul myself onto the slick rocks. Even though Tick-Tock is half the size of the ogre, he is helping Bucket swim to safety. Soon all five of us are perched on the craggy rocks.

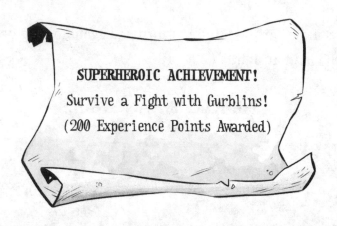

SUPERHEROIC ACHIEVEMENT!
Survive a Fight with Gurblins!
(200 Experience Points Awarded)

Seagulls crowd the rocks like winged rats, snapping up fish that have been stranded by the low tide. The cave entrance yawns above us.

"I think we got ambushed," I say, panting for air.

"I think you are right," says Pan. "If it hadn't been for TickTock, I would have been doomed."

The phibling shrugs. "TickTock does not act like a phibling, but TickTock is still being a phibling," he explains. "Can be breathing air AND water. And can swim good."

"He saved me," says Pan. "When those things grabbed me, I did my best to fight them off. But Tick-Tock is the one who got me free."

"Well, Moxie saved me," I say.

"Saved us all," says Bucket. "Bucket saw orange-hair

girl holding ugly fish goblins out of water. Bucket did it too. Fish goblins not like this. Swam away."

Pan smirks at Moxie. "See? We told you you're smart."

Moxie shakes her head and half grins.

"We told you you're smiling at danger," says Tick-Tock, pointing at her grin.

"We told you we need you," says Bucket.

"Yeah, yeah," she says.

Pan wrings the water out of her robes. Grabbing a long, thin pole from the wreckage, she feels the balance in her hands and nods in satisfaction. Her new bo staff. She turns to Moxie.

"You should get back to the ship," she tells Moxie.

Moxie shakes her head. "Can't."

I turn to her. "What do you mean?"

She shrugs. "Cookie tried to stop me from jumping in," she tells us. "Said as long as I was peeling potatoes for him, I was considered part of the crew. But if I jumped in . . ." She trails off.

"What?" asks TickTock.

"I was on my own," she finishes. "The only way I can come back aboard is with the winning team."

I feel my heart sink. The only reason she put her

hammer down in that dark alley was to save my sorry butt. And now she's done it again. She didn't even want to be here. But she jumped in anyway. To save me.

"I'm so sorry, Moxie." I feel my throat tighten up. "Thank you for saving me. Again. Seriously. I thought I was done for."

"What am I gonna do?" she says. "Let my favorite mage get drowned by gurblins?"

Bucket pats Moxie's hair. "Bucket is glad you come with us."

Moxie laughs. "Thanks, Bucket."

"Me too," I say.

"Me three," says Pan.

"TickTock four."

"All right, all right." Moxie pulls out her sad little sword and wrinkles her nose at it. "You couldn't cut melted butter with this thing."

She chucks the old sword into the sea. Then she pulls out the large wooden spoon and grips and ungrips it with determination. "All right." She nods. "Let's win this thing."

I shake out my robes. "At least we're in the lead," I remind them. "The other teams are still on the boat!"

Moxie's face falls. "Oh dang, Fart."

I turn to her. "What?"

She winces. "The Bad-Breath Bandits and the Fluffy Unicorn Gang jumped in while the gurblins were distracted with you guys."

I can't believe those jerks. "They just left us to fight a pack of gurblins?"

"Worse. They used it to get a head start."

She points to the dripping cave mouth that gapes before us.

"They're already inside the kraken's lair."

CHAPTER TWENTY-FIVE

I imagine the kraken surging out of the dark hole, all webbed feet and gills, gobbling us down into the murky depths forever.

Yep. Super-cheery thoughts.

We all let out a breath. Then Pan leads the way. Into the Hag's Hangnail.

Small crabs scuttle for cover as we approach. We slowly creep down the tunnel into the descending darkness. Ten feet. Twenty. Forty.

We don't even make it fifty feet before we are attacked.

Not by gurblins.

Not by a kraken.

By something far more sinister.
And devious. And cunning.
The Fluffy Unicorn Gang.

AMBUSH!

Clever strategy. Finish us off and they're that much closer to the first-place prize.

The half-orc is on me before I know what has happened. I stumble backward, falling onto the hard stone with a thump. I throw out the first spell that pops into my head.

"*Flimmity-flamesh!*" I cry, casting Cozy Camp. Not a great spell for attacking, but I get lucky. The sudden flare of fire to the face sends her staggering backward. And singes her eyebrows right off.

TickTock leaps forward and shoots webs at the barbarian and the evil-looking dwarf. The hulky barbarian blocks the sticky mass with his club. But the dwarf takes a hit full in the face and tumbles onto his back like a beetle.

The barbarian roars. Recognizing me as a spell-caster, he lurches at me before I can gather my wits.

Joke's on him. I don't have any wits to gather.

I scramble back, desperately flinging my dagger at the huge brute. But it bounces off the wall and plops into a tide pool.

His club flies at my head. But miraculously, something blocks his swing.

It's Moxie. Crisscrossing her tongs and mixing spoon, she halts the barbarian's deadly blow.

PA-CHOW! She gives him a sharp kick to the kneecap, sending him crumpling in pain.

"Look out, Moxie!" I cry, pointing. The archer has drawn her bow and fires right at us.

Moxie turns her back to the arrows, selflessly shielding me from the oncoming flurry.

PING! PING! PING!

Astonishingly, the arrows bounce off her back and clatter uselessly to the floor. I can't believe my eyes. She wears no armor, and yet the deadly arrows simply ricochet off her back . . . her mucky cloak . . . as if it were made of metal.

"I think we know what that magic cloak does now," I tell her.

CLOAK OF THE SHIELD

Protects like armor.

90% magic-infused sagecotton.

10% polyester. For that casual wear-it-anywhere look.

Hand-wash only. Hang-dry.

A huge grin splits her face. She twists the cloak around to cover her chest instead of her back. And with tongs in one hand and spoon in the other, she charges the archer like a rabid crab.

Pan is pummeling the half-orc in the eyes with orbs of salt water.

Bucket is locked in club-to-club combat with the barbarian.

TickTock is finishing off the weakened dwarf.

And the gnoll is charging right at me.

GNOLL   Very slobbery.

Always barking at the mailman.

Not house-trained.

This is it. My chance is here! My time is now! It's time for Mind Control. This flea-bitten mutt will be putty in my hand!

I see murder in his wild eyes. Slobber froths from his mouth in anticipation of the kill. I choke. Panic. I can't recall the complex words to the spell! My hands start to shake. He's almost on me.

So I do what I do best.

I run.

Back to the entrance. Back to the sunlight. Back . . . to the seagulls.

They still scream and squabble in an unruly crowd. Luckily, I speak their language.

"Pfeatherfax-pfuffernutter." The Feather Friend spell settles over my vocal cords. The gnoll is hot on my heels, but I try to focus on the birds.

"Hey! Birdbrains!" I shout at them. Only instead of words, squealing caws erupt from my mouth. Yep. I'm speaking seagull.

They turn my way.

"Want more fish?" I screech.

"More fish! Yes! More fish!" they yammer.

I point to the gnoll. "That dogman has lots of fish in his pockets!"

The seagulls turn their heads hungrily toward the gnoll. This stops him in his tracks.

He tries to flee. But the birds are on him, all flapping feathers and jabbing beaks. And there's no escape when seagulls attack.

I dash back to my friends.

TickTock has completely web-wrapped the unconscious dwarf.

The archer's bow lies snapped on the ground. Her arms fly furiously at Moxie with two cruelly pointed daggers. But she cannot penetrate Moxie's cloak.

Moxie grabs the archer by the nose with her kitchen tongs.

But Moxie doesn't stop it. She drags her by the nose. Back to the cave entrance. And chucks her into the pounding surf.

The half-orc and the barbarian are cornered and outnumbered. But they don't seem to care. The scorched half-orc snarls with hate. The barbarian quivers with fury.

"Just hold on," says Pan calmly. "It doesn't have to end like this."

"Feh," the half-orc spits. "You heard Diremaw. There can only be one winning team."

That's enough for the barbarian. He screams and barrels forward, club raised for a death blow.

"Plaintanitar au musa," I say. Banana peels shoot from my palms, showering the ground in front of him.

His foot hits a banana peel. He slides recklessly forward, arms swinging like pinwheels. Moxie leaps, arm out, clotheslining the barbarian across the neck. He crashes to the floor, sending his club soaring into the air behind him. He skids across the chamber on a sea of banana peels, crumpling against the far wall.

We turn to face the half-orc.

But she has caught the barbarian's club. Right in the noggin.

CHAPTER TWENTY-SIX

The Fluffy Unicorn Gang is kaput.

SUPERHEROIC ACHIEVEMENT!
Defeat Some Sneaky Sailors!
(250 Experience Points Awarded)

Only us and the Bad-Breath Bandits are left.

We all breathe a sigh. "I just love that banana spell, Fart!" Moxie tells me. "It's so adorable!"

Adorable. Just what I was going for.

Bucket scratches his rear end with his club. "Not done yet," he says. "Still don't got the kraken's fathead."

Moxie laughs and shoves the ogre. "Flatbread, not fathead," she says. "You're the fathead."

Bucket smiles. "No. You fathead." He playfully shoves Moxie back.

"Bucket is being right," says TickTock, lighting a torch. "Heroes not out of this yet."

It's impossible to see what creepy-crawlies lie in wait in this ankle-deep water. We make our way down the dark tunnel, wreckage littering the cavern before us. Cargo and equipment from the *Tangerine*.

Timbers jut from the waters like rotten teeth. Pieces of sail flap like long-dead ghosts. I see a corroded frying pan. A pasta strainer. A set of kitchen tongs.

"What's with all the cooking supplies?" I whisper.

"Don't forget," says Pan softly. "Juliette Kidd was a chef. Her ship was basically a floating kitchen."

The utensils are rusted and crusty from their long

sleep in this watery tomb. But something sparkles in the torchlight. Moxie reaches into the murky water, pulling a shiny object from beneath a torn sail.

"It is being a hammer!" cries TickTock.

"It's not a hammer," says Moxie. "It's a silver meat tenderizer. A really nice one!"

THE MEAT TENDERIZER
OF JULIETTE KIDD

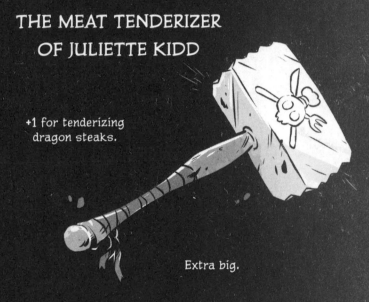

+1 for tenderizing
dragon steaks.

Extra big.

"Look," says Pan, her sharp eyes piercing the dark tunnel before us.

TickTock hoists the torch higher, the light glimmering on rows of gigantic stalagmites. They stretch from the floor, clawing toward the ceiling far above.

But as we creep closer, my eyes adjust.

They're not stalagmites. They're bones.

Moxie rushes forward to examine them. Tucking the silver meat tenderizer into her belt, she reaches into her pack and yanks out a thick book. *Buzzlock's Big Book of Beasts*.

"TickTock is thinking this whole quest is being a bad idea," the phibling says with a gulp. "Lots of big bones here. If the kraken is eating all these creatures, he is swallowing TickTock in one gulp."

"These aren't creatures," says Moxie, eyeing the bones closely. "It's one big creature."

She's right. A single spine, thick as a tree trunk, connects the jutting ribs. But it's been snapped in half like a twig.

Whatever this sea creature was, it was truly massive. Bigger than the *Death Knell* herself. Walking the length of the skeleton, I find Moxie crouched near a skull the size of a boulder.

"Do you know what this is?" she whispers, looking up from her book in awe.

"Isn't it obvious?" I ask fearfully. "Leftovers from the kraken's dinner. And we're next."

Moxie closes the book. "This isn't the skeleton of the kraken's dinner."

Pan shakes her head, confused. "Then what is it?"

Moxie gulps. "This is the skeleton of the kraken."

CHAPTER TWENTY-SEVEN

We gawk at the bones in terrified silence. The *click-clack*ing of spider crabs echoes eerily in the darkness around us. Finally TickTock asks the question we're all wondering.

"What could be snapping a kraken in half like this?"

There's no answer.

My head is spinning. I feel light-headed. I bend down and tuck my head between my knees to stop myself from passing out. Or to kiss my butt goodbye. Whichever is needed first.

"I don't think we can do this," I say.

"What choice do we have?" says Pan calmly. "We

either come out with the Kraken's Flatbread or we don't come out at all."

"Well, that's a depressing thought," I mutter.

"No," she says, her voice echoing in the gloom. "What is truly depressing is that we are enduring all of this not for any worthwhile cause . . . but for the sake of Kevin."

We turn to her. "What do you mean?" asks Moxie.

Pan takes a deep breath and faces us, her pointy eyebrows looming large. "What loyalty do we owe him?" she asks. "He snaps his fingers, gives us a pile of sketchy information, and sends us off into untold danger, hurtling our well-ordered lives into chaos."

Moxie snickers. "I'm not so sure how well-ordered our lives were."

"What are you talking about?" I ask Pan.

"I've simply been thinking," Pan says, smoothing her hair into place. "Perhaps we should forget about Kevin's quest."

"Forgetting Kevin's quest?" asks TickTock.

"Are you kidding me?" I ask.

Pan cocks an eyebrow at us. "We helped Ephemera rid the Sparkly Glade of spindernots. That was a worthwhile quest. We had a plan and executed it with aplomb."

"So this quest isn't worthwhile?" I ask.

Pan bites her lip.

"Kevin is paying us a fat sack of cash," Moxie weighs in. "That seems pretty worthwhile to me."

"Exactly!" I cry. "Plus we told him we'd do it!"

The elf grimaces. "I do not trust the Great and Powerful Kevin."

TickTock wrings his hands nervously. But says nothing.

"If we're not going to trust Kevin, then who should we trust?" I ask in annoyance. "Every pixie that knocks on our door? A bunch of filthy, unruly pirates?"

Pan purses her lips thoughtfully. "I did not say that. Though they are not as unruly as one might think. They are obedient and well organized. There is order beneath the chaos that works in unison to run a tight ship."

"You're defending the pirates?" I cry.

"I am not defending them," Pan clarifies. "I am just hesitant to make the same mistake I made with the muck elves. We should not judge them prematurely."

I think you hit your head when we fell overboard, I tell her.

"You have to admit," she says calmly, "there is something to be said for a well-ordered, shipshape life. Perhaps something like that holds promise for us."

It's official . . . the world has gone loco. Maybe it's the fear of facing the kraken. But I feel like everything is spinning out of control.

Suddenly the words are in my mind. And before I know it, they're on my tongue.

"El sila erin lu e-govaned vin.
Avo garo am man theled!"

Pan's face goes slack. She stares blankly at me.

"You think you're a pirate, Pan?" I cry, shaking. "You're not! We're going to get the Kraken's Flatbread. Get the bedazzler's barf. And take them back to Kevin like we planned. No improvising!"

I can't believe it. I did it. I cast Mind Control.

Pan's pupils swell, filling her eyes. Like black pools. Like shark eyes.

She turns to me. "Avast, me hearties!" she cries. Her

voice sounds gravelly and coarse, not at all like Pan. More like . . . First Mate Tidepool. More like . . . a pirate.

"We'll be plundering this cave and getting that kraken's booty!" she roars. "Or me name isn't Pan the Perilous!"

Moxie grips my shoulder tightly. "What have you done?" she whispers.

CHAPTER TWENTY-EIGHT

"What have you done?" Moxie hisses again.

I think I've turned Pan into a pirate. That's what I've done.

"I . . . I . . . I . . . didn't mean to," I sputter. "She was talking crazy talk. She was . . . I was . . . I was trying to stop her."

"Stop her? How?" demands Moxie. "By using your magic on her? By using your powers on your friend?"

Okay, I have to admit . . . when you say it out loud, it sounds really bad. "It . . . it . . . it was an accident!" I cry, trying to explain. "I just got upset!"

Moxie pushes past me angrily, grabbing Pan by the shoulders. "Pan?" she calls to her. "Pan?"

"That be Pan the Perilous to you, ye cockle-eyed lubber!" Pan roars.

Maybe I misfired the spell. Maybe I misspoke the
incantation. Maybe this magic is just too powerful for
me. Whatever I did, I've really botched this up. I'm
pretty sure things can't get any worse.

Wrong.

Because that's when the screaming starts.

We all turn, weapons drawn.

Screams of panic echo up to us from farther down
the tunnel.

There's an eerie green glow down there, flickering off
the slick walls. Suddenly a figure emerges, feet sloshing
through ankle-deep water. Coming right at us.

It's Weasel. And he's fleeing for his life.

"Run, you idiots!" he cries. "It's down there!"

He dashes past us, back toward the entrance.

"What's down there?" Bucket yells.

But Weasel doesn't stop to share. "It has them!" he
screams. And he disappears into the darkness.

Our heads swivel to peer back down the tunnel. Slop-
ing fifty more feet, the passage rounds a bend. There's
something down there, waiting for us. Something
glow-y.

The screaming has stopped abruptly. The silence is more terrifying than the screams.

"Arrggg!" roars Pan. "Methinks our quarry be dead ahead! Unto the breach, me hearties!" She grips her staff and charges down the tunnel.

Moxie shoots me a frosty glare. "This is not over," she says. And chases after Pan, the ogre and phibling right behind her.

I'm petrified. Whatever is down there snapped a kraken in half. Whatever is down there sent Weasel running for his life. Whatever is down there has probably killed the rest of the Bad-Breath Bandits.

And yet I'd rather face ten of whatever is down there than see Moxie look at me like that again. I force myself to put one soggy foot in front of the other and run after my friends.

Pan has halted at the opening to a huge chamber. Pools fill the wide cavern, leftovers from the retreating tide. The entire chamber flickers with that ghostly green light. We immediately spot the source of the light. My blood turns cold in my veins.

The broken hull of a ship stands looming before us like a watchtower.

Yep, I said STANDS. Because this shipwreck has legs.

It has arms. It even seems to have a face. Green ghost light pulses from two porthole eyes. And there, high across one of the splintered boards, I see a word written in faded gold lettering.

Tangerine.

CHAPTER TWENTY-NINE

The wreck shifts its position, staring at us like some giant wooden zombie. Raising its barnacle-encrusted arms, it lets out a deafening roar.

ROOOOOOOOOOAAAAAAAAAR!

We scatter in terror behind the nearest rock. Echoes of the bone-chilling roar bounce off the cavern walls. "I think there might be some pee leaking out of me right now," I say softly. "I can't tell for sure. My pants are still wet."

"Well blow me down!" whispers Pan the Perilous, peeking out at the creature in awe. "That there beastie be Juliette Kidd's ship! The *Tangerine*! What scurvy witchcraft be this?"

Moxie quickly opens the book that's still in her hand. "I think I know," Moxie says. She looks up nervously from the pages. "It's a golem."

GOLEM

A creature animated by a powerful sorcerer.

Can be made of stone, wood, metal, or even flesh.

Possesses untold strength.

Will follow the final orders of their creator, even once the creator has died.

I risk a peek. The shipwreck creature just stands there. But something tells me that could change any moment. "How did Juliette Kidd's ship turn into a golem?"

TickTock tugs on my robes. "Remember Diremaw's

story? Right before being pulled down into the deep, Juliette Kidd was casting a powerful spell to preserve her flatbread."

Moxie nods. "Maybe her spell didn't just preserve the flatbread. Maybe it preserved the whole ship."

"Not just that," says Bucket. "It made ship come alive!"

"Well I'll be a fluffy narwhal!" nods Pan. "That it did!"

Her face splits into a crooked grin. She excitedly spins her staff overhead. I can see the recklessness in her eyes.

I've created a monster.

ROOOOOOOOOAAAAAAAAAR!

And so did Juliette Kidd. The Magician of the Kitchen's evil creation bellows a challenge to us.

In that moment, time seems to stop. And everything is clear.

Magic is great. But it's also an uncontrollable force of nature. Even a powerful mage like Juliette Kidd can accidentally create a monster if they're not careful.

Pan the Perilous shoots me a jaunty wink and does something the real Pan would never do.

She doesn't assess the situation. She doesn't make a

plan. She screams, "DEATH OR GLORY, ME BUCKOS!" and starts to launch herself into battle.

For once, I know exactly what to do. I grab Pan's bola and spin it around her arm, binding her temporarily to Moxie. Then I grit my teeth, willing myself to action.

"Distract it for me," I tell Moxie. "I need to get close."

"Fart!" Moxie cries, reaching for me. "No! That thing will pulverize you!"

But I'm already gone. I splish-splash softly through the pools to the edge of the cavern, skirting the horrific creature.

My last bit of magic was a major screwup. I'm determined that this next spell won't be. I'm sticking with a nice simple one that I know by heart.

Gas Attack.

TINK! TINK! TINK!

It's Moxie, banging on the stone with her new meat tenderizer, trying to keep the golem focused on them.

"HEY!" yells Bucket, waving his arms. "Over here!"

"YOO-HOO!" says TickTock. He waves his butt at the thing.

The creature raises its arms and lets loose another bellow.

I'm close enough to see the texture of the creature's splintered wooden legs.

I reach out. I have to touch it. That's what sometimes makes this spell so useless. But not today.

I place my hand on the rough wood and utter the words that will turn this creature into a cloud of gas.

"Flatulencia."

And suddenly . . . nothing happens.

Well, I shouldn't say nothing.

The creature peers down at me with its glowing port-hole eyes.

And it kicks me.

"Fart!" Moxie gasps, dashing over to me. "Are you okay?"

I crack my neck, feeling for broken bones. But I seem

to be in one piece. Everyone turns toward the shipwreck golem, expecting it to smash us flat. But it holds its position. Maybe it can't attack until we come into the chamber.

"Why didn't that work?" I ask. "It should turn any living creature I touch into a fart!"

"Ship not alive," suggests Bucket.

"He's right," says Moxie. "It's just been magically animated."

Oh. Well, crud on a cracker.

And then we hear it.

"HAHAHAHAHA!" The insane laughter echoes around the cavern, a raspy cackle that sends a frozen shiver of fear racing down my spine. "No," says the eerie voice. "The ship is not alive. And neither am I."

Up on the head of the shipwreck creature, near the captain's wheel. A bony hand emerges. Dragging with it . . . a body. A skeletal body.

Ribs show through the torn chef's coat it wears. Wiry hair sprouts from the skull like crabgrass. Green light peers down upon us from within the empty eye sockets.

"Look, *Tangerine*," the skeleton hisses. "More thieves. Come to take my scrumptious flatbread."

My mind races. To Kevin's Monster Museum. To his bedazzler statue. To his minotaur statue. To his . . .

"Well I'll be a jolly roger," mutters Pan.

My knees go weak.

Because this is Juliette Kidd.

But she's no longer Juliette Kidd.

The Magician of the Kitchen . . . is a lich.

CHAPTER THIRTY

TickTock grips my robes in terror. "Something is telling TickTock that Juliette Kidd's magic did not just preserve her ship and her flatbread."

"It preserved her, too," Moxie whispers, her throat catching. "She's a lich!"

"So," says the lich. "More thieves here for my flatbread? I can't say I blame you. It was my greatest creation. Flaky. Golden. The perfect blend of seasoning. Just a touch of cheese." The lich seems lost in the memory. "Sounds delicious, doesn't it?" it asks playfully.

I nod. We all do.

"But thanks to that despicable kraken, I'll never taste

it." It gnashes its teeth together. "I'll never taste anything again!"

Pan steps forward cockily, twirling her makeshift bo staff. "How sad ye story be," she sneers at the lich. "Makes me want to go boo-hoo in me grog!"

"Pan!" Moxie hisses. She shakes her head in anger. "Fart, I could just throttle you."

I reach out to tug my elf friend back. "Pan! Stop!" I plead. "Please!"

But Pan ignores me. "Seems a crying shame to let such a tasty morsel go to waste," she calls to the lich. "Why not let Pan the Perilous take that wee flatbread off your hands?"

"NO!" roars the lich, stomping its bony foot. "If I can't taste it, no one can!"

Pan shrugs at us with a jaunty grin. "Nobody can say I didn't try to reason with the beastie!" She turns, lets out a bloodcurdling howl, and leaps toward the creature.

"Elf-girl!" TickTock cries.

Moxie grips her meat tenderizer tightly. "So what's the plan, Fart?"

"I don't know," I say helplessly. "Pan is usually the one with the plan."

"Yeah," she says, shooting me an angry glare. "I know."

My mind races. "Moxie, tell me everything you know about liches!"

The anger and panic leave her as she thumbs through the book in her hand. "They are powerful spell-casters. They can mortally wound you just with their freezing touch. Only powerful magic or silver weapons can hurt them . . ."

"Silver weapons!" cries TickTock, his eyes lighting up.

"I know!" says Moxie in frustration. "If only we had a silver weapon!"

"Hammer-girl!" yells TickTock, pointing. "You are having silver right there in your hand!"

Moxie drops the book and lifts the meat tenderizer. A wicked grin passes over her face. With a bellow, she charges the golem.

The wooden creature swipes madly at Pan, but the elf dodges the anchor-tipped arm and leaps onto the golem, climbing toward the lich. The lich lobs magic arrows at the elf, but even in pirate mode Pan is too nimble for words.

TickTock tries to web the golem's wooden legs together, but the creature is too strong, and the webs tear away like tissue. Bucket gets a wooden arm to the gut and goes flying.

I stay put. Doing nothing. I hate myself for it. For standing there uselessly and watching my friends do battle. But after the last kick in the ribs, I'm wary. Plus what could I really do?

I could hurl a few Magic Missiles. It might do a little damage.

Gas Attack is worthless against the nonliving.

Even Feather Friend won't help. No birds down here.

Pan leaps onto the shoulder of the shipwreck golem. Moxie pounds the golem viciously, sending wood chips flying.

I look down. Moxie's book lies at my feet, open to the page on liches. I snatch it up and skim Buzzlock's notes.

Liches can cast powerful magic.

Their freezing touch can cause mortal wounds.

Only silver weapons can hurt them.

They keep their souls in a soul silo, an object of special significance to them. Gaining possession of the soul silo weakens the lich.

Wait! *Soul silo.*

I hear a roar of pain and look up from the page.

"PAN!" I start to run to her side, but now the golem has Moxie in its grasp.

It raises her into the air. She beats her meat tenderizer brutally on the wooden doors that cover its chest, the spiky utensil embedding into the wood and

sticking fast. She tugs in frustration, biceps bulging, trying to free her only weapon.

CRAAAACKKK!

The hinges of the door rip away. Wood splinters as

the door drops to the wet stone below. A ray of blinding green light billows forth from the creature's chest. And I see it.

The source of the green glow. The heart of the golem. Our prize.

THE KRAKEN'S FLATBREAD

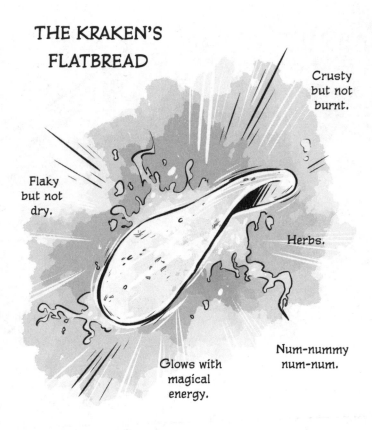

Crusty but not burnt.

Flaky but not dry.

Herbs.

Num-nummy num-num.

Glows with magical energy.

It's the flatbread.

An object of special significance to the lich. Of course! *The flatbread is the soul silo.*

"PREPARE FOR OBLIVION, THIEF!" roars the lich. The golem tightens its grip on Moxie, and she screams out in pain.

Water sloshes against my leg.

Ocean water.

Crud on a cracker. The tide is coming back in.

Bucket has limped over to help Pan. She's wounded but conscious. Thank goodness.

I have to do something to help Moxie. To save her. Even if I'm a pathetic fighter. I won't just stand here. I must defend my friends.

I reach for the silver dagger on my belt. Gone. Lost in the fight with the gnoll. But that's when I feel them. Tucked into the inner pocket of my robes.

My magic scrolls.

I forgot all about them. Three scrolls of powerful magic. Squiddly-Diddly. Stone to String Cheese. And Barlowe's Belching Bubble.

Powerful spells, beyond my ability. But according to Kevin, all I have to do is read the words.

Unfurling a parchment, I speak the words on the page:

"Shirak cecestia.
Crustasea manos.
Tentacula spectacula.
Octaciencia splendiferencia!"

My hands. They feel weird.

"That's right, *Tangerine!*" shouts the lich. "Squeeze my enemies to pulp!"

Moxie releases a howl of pain as the scroll burns to ashes in my fingers.

Suddenly giant pink strands shoot from my arms. They wave around, writhing like seaweed.

No. Not seaweed.

Tentacles.

I have become a giant squid.

CHAPTER THIRTY-ONE

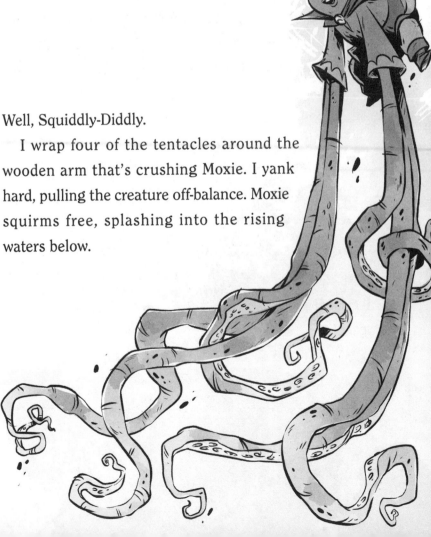

Well, Squiddly-Diddly.

I wrap four of the tentacles around the wooden arm that's crushing Moxie. I yank hard, pulling the creature off-balance. Moxie squirms free, splashing into the rising waters below.

I have absolute control of these squid arms. And massive strength.

But the golem is strong too. Strong enough to rip a kraken in half. It tugs against my tentacles, trying to regain its footing.

"Well!" cackles the lich. "Looks like we have another magician in the kitchen!"

The golem swings its anchor arm down, severing one of my tentacles with a *squelch*. I feel no pain, but now I'm one tentacle short of a full squid. Luckily I have seven more.

Reaching out, I wrap two around the anchor arm.

Two more grab a leg.

One clutches the other leg. And I

pull with all my strength. Normal Fart is pretty weak.
But Squiddly-Diddly Fart is mighty.

The lich slings a lightning bolt at me. I manage to
block it with a tentacle, and it absorbs
into the rubbery flesh with a fizzle.

"Moxie! TickTock! Bucket!"
I roar to my friends.
"Get the soul
silo!"

"Get what now?" asks Bucket.

"The flatbread!" I cry, straining to hold the golem at bay. "Once we possess the flatbread, we'll be able to destroy the lich!"

TickTock's eyes glow with understanding. Already the phibling is sticky-walking up the golem with his gecko-like feet. Making a beeline for the golem's chest. For the Kraken's Flatbread.

But the lich sees what we're up to.

"NO!" it roars. Lightning crackles from its fingertips. TickTock leaps deftly aside, barely dodging the scorching bolts.

Reaching into the golem's chest, the phibling tugs. The flatbread is almost as big as he is.

The golem roars, wrenching itself from my Squiddly grip. "Hurry, TickTock!"

The phibling grunts, pulling with all his might.

POP!

All eyes follow his descent as he drops into the rising waters. Furious, the lich sends a barrage of green glowing arrows exploding into the water where the phibling fell. For a long moment, time seems to freeze in place.

But then TickTock emerges, the glowing flatbread held over his head.

SUPERHEROIC ACHIEVEMENT!
Snag a Lich's Soul Silo!
(400 Experience Points Awarded)

"HOW DARE YOU!" bellows the lich, contorting in pain.

But its voice has lost some of its power. The light in its vacant eye sockets has dimmed. The lich has been weakened.

"Now, Moxie!" I cry, gripping the golem with all my might. "We have the soul silo!"

"Hammer-girl!" yells TickTock. "It is being silver hammer time!"

Moxie clenches the meat tenderizer, glaring at the lich. "Hold that golem tight, Fart!" she cries.

"I'm trying!" I shout, my tentacles taut with the strain.

The lich knows we're coming for it. And it knows how to stop us.

By taking out the one thing that's holding back its precious *Tangerine*.

Me.

"*Acerak con sagavel chelamshathasalmago-ritharr!*" the lich roars. Its hands, spread wide, glow red with terrible power.

METEOR STORM!

Bucket grabs the huge wooden door and shields Pan and TickTock with it.

Moxie takes cover under her magical cloak.

I dive under the waist-high water, pulling my tentacle arms over me as protection from the deadly barrage. Holding my breath, I sense the fiery meteors splashing around me. The water bubbles with churning heat. I hold my breath until my lungs feel like they'll explode. Only then do I burst from the water.

Three more of my tentacles have been scorched beyond

recognition. Miraculously, I'm not a charcoal briquette. But I'm four tentacles down. This lich is turning my precious squid arms into sushi.

"Bucket!" Moxie roars. "Get me up there!"

Holding the scorched door over his head, Bucket dashes to Moxie. "Bucket got you, orange-hair girl!"

With a flying leap, Moxie springs onto the door and Bucket flings her sky-ward.

With the last of my strength, I coil my remaining four arms around the golem's wooden limbs. And I tug.

"Hurry, Moxie! Time's up!"

Whatever magic binds this golem together is on the verge of giving way. The ship splinters under my suckers. But I feel something else, too. A tingling in my arms.

My spell is wearing off.

The water is up to my chest. And rising.

The lich faces Moxie. It points a finger at my friend. And it starts to utter the spell that will destroy Moxie once and for all.

"*Flameo c'est baller*—acck!"

"Eat wood, ye bony blowhard!" Pan cries. Hurt as she is, Pan has climbed up the golem's other side. She smashes her driftwood staff across the lich's skull, shattering the stick to splinters.

The lich latches on to Pan's arm with a bony grasp. A bloodcurdling shriek of pain escapes Pan's lips at the creature's freezing touch. She falls, dropping limply into the rising tide.

"Why bother, mortals?" asks the lich. "Soon my chamber will be underwater once again. You will be dead. And I will reclaim my flatbread from your corpses with a smile."

"Try smiling without a head!" howls Moxie. Swinging the silver meat tenderizer, Moxie roars with all her might.

KRACKEROOSKI!

The skull flies from its skeletal body.

Pulling an arm free from my weakening grasp, the golem catches the skull in midair. From its closed fist comes a hysterical high-pitched laugh.

The golem's wooden palm opens.

The skull of Juliette Kidd smiles.

"YOU FOOLS!" the skull croaks. "Severing my head will not end the Magician of the Kitchen! And now my sweet *Tangerine* will crush your skulls to dust."

The shipwreck golem is pulling free from my weakening grasp. I'm almost completely underwater.

"You're not the only cook in this kitchen, sister," Moxie says with a grin. "And crushed skull sounds like a recipe for success!"

The eye sockets glow no more. Because they have been smashed to smithereens.

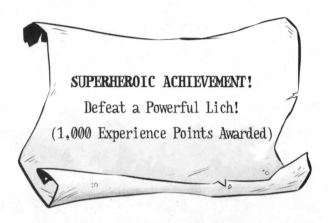

SUPERHEROIC ACHIEVEMENT!
Defeat a Powerful Lich!
(1,000 Experience Points Awarded)

I feel a shudder go through the shipwreck. With my last ounce of Squiddly strength, I grit my teeth. I strain so hard, I fear for the condition of my underpants.

Timbers crack. Sails rip. Beams break.

Moxie leaps from the hand of the golem, diving into the rising waters.

With a final heave, the ship tears in half.

Wreckage rains into the water below.

Juliette Kidd and the *Tangerine* are finally at rest.

CHAPTER THIRTY-TWO

Bucket has plucked Pan from the surging waters. She's barely conscious and shivers with cold.

TickTock tugs Moxie from the water, onto the floating wreckage of the golem.

My tentacles tingle, shrinking back into normal arms.

"Fart?" Pan calls to me weakly. "Did you . . . did you turn me into a pirate?"

"Pan?" I swim over to her, grasping her in my arms.

"I think your stupid spell is starting to wear off." Her voice is mostly back to normal. She no longer has those black shark eyes. Her one eyebrow is cocked at me sternly.

Oh, thank goodness.

"Pan!" cries Moxie with relief.

"I . . . I . . . I'm so sorry, Pan," I begin.

Bucket props her up. "I can't believe you did that," Pan moans. "You turned me into a pirate."

"I know," I groan.

"I was there, inside my head, but I had no control," she says in a shuddering breath. "It was like being back in the muck-elf prison, but this time the prison was my mind."

There's nothing for me to say. I hang my head, ashamed to meet her gaze. I wouldn't be surprised if she never speaks to me again.

"Look at me," says Pan. My vision wobbles with tears as I look into her eyes. "If you EVER use your magic against one of us again, I will NEVER forgive you."

Moxie grabs my shoulder. "That goes double for me," she says sternly.

"I promise," I tell them. "No more Mind Control for me. I'm so sorry." But then Pan's words sink in. I look up hopefully. "Does that mean you forgive me?"

She quirks an eyebrow and smirks. "Aye, matey," she says. "This time."

Moxie lets out a whoop of relief. "Woo-hoo!" she

cheers. "We got Pan back! And thanks to TickTock, we got the Kraken's Flatbread!"

"We are getting the flatbread as a team!" the phibling says, beaming.

"Don't matter, friends," says Bucket, pointing. "We all out of time."

He's right. The rising waters have completely flooded the tunnel that leads back to the entrance. We are trapped. We bob to the ceiling as the salty waves quickly rise.

I can't believe it. After everything we've gone through, it ends like this.

"Guys . . ." In these final moments, I want to express to them how much they mean to me. How glad I am that we're ending things as friends. But I don't have to.

"I know, Fart," says Moxie. "Me too."

There's only four feet of air left.

"Same here," says Pan.

Three feet of air left.

Moxie turns to the phibling with realization. "Tick-Tock! You can breathe water! You should take the flat-bread and get out of here!"

TickTock looks at the glowing flatbread and shakes his head. "TickTock not leaving his friends."

Bucket nods. "Bucket neither."

Two feet left.

I struggle to stay afloat. I feel my spellbook weighing me down. I reach to unhook it. To release it from dragging me to the bottom too early. But my hand wraps around something else.

My two remaining scrolls. One containing a spell called Stone to String Cheese.

And one called Barlowe's Belching Bubble.

One foot of air left.

I rip the scroll from my robes, unfurl it, and quickly read the words.

"Globulealis oxyhyrdenium.
Bubbalencia effervencia.
Surrondem au'floatencia!"

Zero feet of air left.

We are submerged. Panic fills Moxie's eyes. But deep in my gut, I feel a gurgling. A churning. Gas burbles up my throat, emerging from my mouth in a huge . . .

"BRAAAAAWWWWPPP!"

A belching bubble of air issues forth from my mouth,

leaving me and my friends surrounded in a burp-scented bubble. Our own private lifesaving hamster ball.

SUPERHEROIC ACHIEVEMENT!
Save Your Friends from a
Watery Grave!
(250 Experience Points Awarded)

CHAPTER THIRTY-THREE

"Fart, you sweet baby mage!" says Moxie.

I am a sweet baby mage. No truer words were ever spoken.

We are a mash of legs, arms, and heads, all squashed

into the six-foot bubble that surrounds me. But we can breathe.

"We is saved!" cheers Bucket.

"Only for the moment," I say. Our ball of air is being held at the top of the water-filled cavern. But if we don't figure a way out of here, we're finished when this spell wears off.

"Don't worry, friends," says Ticktock with a determined look. "TickTock is being an excellent swimmer."

Giving the flatbread to Moxie, the phibling pushes against the wall of the bubble, easily passing through, into the waters beyond. He gives us a thumbs-up. It's a weird sensation. I feel like a goldfish in a bowl.

TickTock grabs the bubble. And starts swimming.

He's a great little swimmer. But he is wee and our bubble is big.

Ticktock pushes a button on his belt. Out pops his Marvelous Spinning Pinwheel of Coolness. Not only does this gizmo get rid of outhouse stench like a champ, but the phibling slides his belt backward and his little propeller zoomy-zooms us nicely through the water.

Thank goodness for this little guy.

We pass the bones of the kraken. The spot where the Fluffy Unicorn Gang ambushed us. I see daylight ahead, coming from the cave entrance. TickTock pushes us through and our bubble bobs to the surface, bouncing on the choppy waves next to the Hag's Hangnail.

We made it. The bubble dissolves as the fresh air hits us.

Everyone pulls themselves onto the slippery rocks. Alive. I can't believe it.

I yank the phibling into a hug. "TickTock, you were amazing."

"It is no problem!" TickTock says with a shrug. "Tick-Tock is being Kevin's number one helper-dude. Is good at being a helper."

"No," says Pan weakly. "You are not a helper."

"Not a helper?" The phibling looks concerned.

Moxie shakes her head. "No way," she says, holding up the flatbread. "You're the one who got the soul silo! We never would have defeated the lich without you."

I chime in. "You're the one who got us out of the cave. We would have drowned without you."

"You saved me when the gurblins had me," says Pan softly. "You are braver than half the monks I knew back at Krakentop Academy."

"You're no helper," I tell him. "You're a hero."

TickTock's eyes go wide. "Like Hammer-girl? Like elf-girl? Like Fart-boy?"

"A baby hero," I say with a giggle. "But still a hero."

TickTock gulps solemnly. "When TickTock's village made TickTock leave, TickTock thought he would never find a place to belong. Was happy to become helper to Kevin, even though Kevin is bossy and eats too many eggs and keeps TickTock around only for his good inventions and breakfast-making skills."

He looks us over. Something has shifted in him. "But now TickTock has new family. And now TickTock knows what he is."

I choke. Not because of TickTock's super-moving speech. But because there's suddenly a dagger at my throat.

"You're a hero," says a greasy voice in my ear. "I'm a hero. We're all heroes."

It's Weasel.

"You made it," he hisses. "I'm so glad. Unfortunately there can only be one winning team." I hear the smile in his voice. He's so pleased with himself. I can smell his rank breath. The guy needs to seriously up his dental-hygiene game. "Now hand over that flat[...] or the mage gets skewered."

Mustering her strength, Pan stands up tall.

TickTock pulls out his dagger with a *shing*.

Bucket lifts his club onto his shoulder.

And Moxie grips and ungrips her silver meat tenderizer.

I see it in their eyes. There's no way they are giving up this time. I'm so glad.

"You tell them, mage!" Uncertainty creeps into Weasel's voice. The dagger presses sharply into my throat. "You tell them to drop their weapons and give me that bit of treasure!"

I clear my throat. "Hammer-girl?"

Moxie tightens her grip on her meat tenderizer. "Yes?"

"Oh good," I say with a grin. "You know who you are again."

I snap my fingers. I twirl my wrists. I place a hand on Weasel's arm.

"Say it!" he hisses.

I say it. Just three words. It's just a baby spell. A Simple Suggestion, really. "Let me go."

He takes my Simple Suggestion. He releases his grip. And I duck.

Moxie's meat tenderizer flies through the air, slamming him hard in the chest. I hear the air *oof* from his lungs. His arms pinwheel, but the force of Moxie's throw is too much. He topples backward into the raging surf.

I reach out and snatch Moxie's meat tenderizer right before it plops into the deep.

Weasel splashes and squawks in the churning tide. I sigh and turn to my friends. They all glare at Weasel with distaste. And then Pan does it. She grabs a long strand of seaweed from the rocks. She coils it as good as any pirate could. And she throws the end to the frantically splashing Weasel.

HELP ME!

I'M NOT A GOOD SWIMMER!

He grabs the seaweed with relief. And then I see a dark sheer pass over his face. A look that says we're going to regret helping him.

But that look quickly changes to panic. Because now the gurblins have him.

They swarm him. Dozens of them.

Pan pulls hard on the strands, trying to tug the helpless guy from the frothing waters. But it's too late. The rope of seaweed goes limp. The frothing water calms.

The gurblins are gone. Down into the murky deep. And so is Weasel.

"I guess that's the end of the Bad-Breath Bandits," says Moxie.

"You know what this means?" asks Pan. "We did it. We got the Kraken's Flatbread. And we lived to tell the tale."

She's right. But our quest is far from complete.

Moxie holds out her hand. "Hey, thanks for saving my hammer, Fart."

I look at the silver tool in my hand. "I thought it was a meat tenderizer," I say, raising an eyebrow at her.

"Don't be silly, Fart," she says with a huge grin. "This is obviously a hammer."

CHAPTER THIRTY-FOUR

We stand victorious on the deck of the *Death Knell*.

Pirates cheer for us.

Cookie roars his approval.

Even Ferny gets in on the action. "Don't worry! You'll always be losers in my book!"

Gosh, I hate that plant.

"WELL DONE!" roars First Mate Tidepool. "The captain awaits news of your return in his chambers. Come, lads and lassies! Your reward is nigh!"

But Moxie looks down at her soggy, stained apron. "Give me a minute," she says. "I need to run to the kitchen. I can't go in front of the captain looking like this."

Oh no. Not back to the kitchen. Not back to the potatoes.

"MAKE HASTE!" the gnome roars after her. "Captain Diremaw doesn't like to be kept waiting!"

Moxie dashes belowdecks. Two minutes later, she emerges.

She doesn't wear a filthy apron any longer. She doesn't wear a clean apron. She's wearing her armor. Her new silver hammer gleams from her belt.

"Hammer-girl!" cheers TickTock.

"Orange-hair girl!" exclaims Bucket.

Pan and I breathe a sigh of relief. "Moxie," we say in unison.

"Wait a second, lass!" says Cookie in disappointment. "What happened to your apron?"

She grins. "Apron? I'm a warrior. Why would a warrior wear an apron?"

SUPERHEROIC ACHIEVEMENT!
Regain Your Self-Confidence!
(300 Experience Points Awarded)

She holds aloft the Kraken's Flatbread. It no longer glows green, as though being back above the surface has freed it from its protective shell.

"Well!" roars Tidepool. "Now that we're all changed and tidy, can we kindly go see the captain?"

She holds open the door, and we enter the quarters of Diremaw the Dread. Golden objects sparkle from every corner. The glass domes of Diremaw's precious collection glimmer.

But the bedazzler sits on his cushy chair, looking over a map. "I guess we've wasted enough time here, Ms. Tidepool," he says. "The tide is high. Let us make sail. I was foolish to think these recruits could recover that precious..."

But now his sniffer is going. He smells something. And that something is still-warm, perfectly preserved flatbread. As fresh as the moment it came out of the oven.

Realization hits the bedazzler as he turns his hideous eye upon us.

"The Skullduggery Crew has returned, Captain," says Ms. Tidepool.

Diremaw floats from his chair over to where we stand. "You did it?!" he cries with disbelief.

"Aye, Captain," says Pan.

His huge orb of a body splits into an enormous smile. "Well done, Skullduggery Crew! You shall have a place of honor on the crew of the *Death Knell*!"

"Thank ye, Captain," Pan says. I shoot her a look. "It will be our honor."

"I look forward to hearing all about your adventures within the Hag's Hangnail!" cries the bedazzler. "But first things first!"

Moxie steps forward holding the steaming flatbread. Diremaw inhales deeply. "I have waited for this moment for many an age. Today I taste the legendary flatbread of Juliette Kidd!"

He looks over the perfectly flaky crust. The gooey melted cheese. The roasted tomatoes with just a hint of char. The sprinkling of fresh green herbs. It is truly a culinary treasure.

And then he takes a huge bite.

"Mmmmmmm," moans the bedazzler, slowly chewing. "It's so flaky. It's so tender. It's so . . ."

Sniiiff

His chewing slows. "There's an odd flavor in there. It's not the tomato. That is prepared to perfection. It's not the blend of fourteen cheeses. That is exquisitely balanced. But there's something else. Something not quite right..."

A look of concern crosses his face. He coughs, spewing crumbs from his massive mouth. He's turning a little green around the cheeks. "OH MY GOSH!" he cries in horror. "I know what it is! It's...it's... it's..."

Moxie is the only one quick enough to react. She grabs a golden urn and holds it under the hurling bedazzler's mouth.

SUPERHEROIC ACHIEVEMENT!
Collect a Bedazzler's Barf!
(1,000 Experience Points Awarded)

The rest of us back away.

Finally the retching stops.

The bedazzler clears his throat. "I'm sorry you lot had to witness that! Give me a moment to myself."

"Aye, Captain!" says Tidepool in shock.

We are ushered to the door. "Curse you, Juliette Kidd!" roars the bedazzler. "How could you? A master chef such as yourself! How could you cover your precious flatbread with the green demon weed? How could you cook with—"

The door closes. We don't hear the rest.

But Moxie finishes for him. She puts the lid on the steaming urn of bedazzler barf.

CHAPTER THIRTY-FIVE

I always said it. Moxie is smart. Whether she believes it or not.

"You did that?" I ask Moxie.

She just grins from ear to ear. "What can I say? I'm a terrible cook."

Pan grips Moxie's shoulder fondly. "It's good to see you back to your old self again."

"You too," Moxie says with a big smile. She holds up her silver mallet. "I guess I felt like my hammer was the one thing I had left of Master Redmane. But as I was smashing that lich skull, I realized . . . Master Redmane taught me that move. Anytime I wallop a baddie or splatter a monster, he's there with me."

TickTock grabs Moxie in a hug. "Yay! Hammer-girl has returned!"

Moxie giggles sheepishly. "I'm not all the way there yet. But I'll get there. One step at a time."

One step at a time. I run my hand across my spell-book. The well-worn pages at the front of the book. The smoother less-used ones in the back. And I decide then and there . . . I'm going to hang out in the front of the book for now.

Suddenly bells are ringing. A loud voice cries down from the crow's nest. "Merchant ship! Off the starboard bow!"

First Mate Tidepool runs to the rail. She pulls out a spyglass and peers through it. "Merchant ship, indeed. Nice fat one too. She'll be bulging with treasure, ripe for the picking." She hands the spyglass to Pan. "Get ready, Skullduggery Crew. Your first act of piracy awaits!"

The tiny first mate dashes off, barking orders at the crew to weigh the anchor and trim the midmast and other sailor thingies that I don't understand.

I look at Pan nervously as she peers through the spy-glass. "When we were in there with Diremaw, you said it would be an honor to be part of his crew."

"Yes," she says, gazing into the horizon.

"You were just faking, right?" I ask. "You're not still a pirate, are you?"

She turns to look at me. "What do you think, matey?"

I take a breath. The sluggish merchant ship is drawing nearer and nearer as we gain on our prey. "I think you like boats. You like the order of a crew working together. And I think you're good at this boat thing. It suits you."

She shoots me a swarthy grin. "Right ye are, me hearty."

I keep going. "But I know you. You are logical. And good and kind. Pan the Perilous would never have thrown a rope to Weasel. Only the real Pan would do that."

She leans in. "Then I think you have your answer," she says with a smirk. "See, Fart? You don't need a powerful spell like Mind Control."

"You see the best in your friends," chimes in Moxie. "Even when they don't see it themselves."

Pan grips my shoulders. "That will always be your most powerful magic."

TickTock yanks on Moxie's magic cloak. "TickTock is not meaning to break up this touching moment, but we are almost at the merchant ship!"

253

As if to underscore his words, Diremaw floats to the rail overlooking the main deck. He's looking less green. He gauges the position of the setting sun. "It's almost six o'clock, me hearties! Do your captain proud and we'll be feasting by suppertime!"

"HOORAY FOR DIREMAW THE DREAD!!!"

TickTock bounces nervously from one foot to the other. "Oh no! What are we going to do?"

Moxie grips and ungrips her hammer as she gazes at the fearful faces on the merchant ship. "We're going to do what heroes do, TickTock."

TickTock puffs out his chest and draws his dagger. "We are going to help those merchants!"

"Exactly," says Pan.

"Bucket want to help too," the ogre chimes in. "Plus Bucket go where orange-hair girl go."

"You better get going," Pan says. "I'll meet you over there." She turns and heads the other way.

"Wait!" I cry. "Where are you going?"

She adjusts her jade hair clip and shoots us a jaunty wink. "It's almost six o'clock. And Pan the Perilous has an idea."

CHAPTER THIRTY-SIX

"Prepare to board!" roars First Mate Tidepool.

I grab the nearest free rope. I climb to the top of the rail. And I awkwardly swing over to the merchant vessel.

Moxie, TickTock, and Bucket land right next to me. The merchants look terrified. They think they're all going to die. And Diremaw isn't helping matters.

"You're all going to die!" he roars from the other ship. But then he sees us. Pride fills his voice. "Learn from the Skullduggery Crew, lads!" he calls to his pirates. "Watch them set the example!"

I turn to the men and women before us. Little kids hide behind their moms and dads. These are simple people, just trying to get from one place to another.

I reach out to the nearest merchant. "We're here to help you," I tell him.

"Get us out of here!" Moxie shouts. "We'll try to hold the pirates off!"

The merchant looks confused. But he runs off to sloop the poop deck or whatever thing gets this tub moving. We turn back to the *Death Knell*.

The pirates pause, waiting. I realize they're watching to see what we do. These new heroic crewmates who braved the Hag's Hangnail and lived to tell the tale.

I don't keep them waiting. "*Flimmity-flamesh*," I say. Cozy Camp. The first spell on the first page of the first section of my spellbook.

One of the ropes catches fire and burns away in a pirate's hand.

"*Flimmity-flamesh*." Another rope gone.

"*Flimmity-flamesh*." And another.

In less than a minute, all the pirate ropes have been burned away.

Diremaw's smile evaporates. His huge head purples as the realization dawns on him . . . we've betrayed him. Rage distorts his features. His gemstones, glittering and rich in the candlelight of his quarters, now look gaudy and cheap in the sunlight. I'd even call them tacky if they hadn't just started shooting death beams and disintegration rays at us.

"DON'T JUST STAND THERE GAPING LIKE A BASKET OF HADDOCK!" he roars to his crew. "GET THEM!"

With no ropes to swing on, the pirates pull out long planks and lay them across the gap between the two ships.

The battle is on.

I shoot a Magic Missile at a goblin pirate. He dodges it, plummeting off the plank into the sea below.

"BUCKET!" I yell. "Knock down those planks!"

The little ogre roars and starts bashing planks with his club. Several fall into the water, taking pirates with them.

But the pirates keep coming. TickTock fires his web capsules at several of them. A red-skinned orc gets web-tangled and plunges into the deep. But several others make it across.

Moxie lets out a roar and charges them with her silver hammer. A burly pirate cowers at her ferocity and jumps overboard. But a huge troll moves in to replace him. Moxie locks hammer and sword with him.

I zap a Magic Missile at the troll attacking Moxie. He lets out a howl and flies backward into the surf. I cast another Cozy Camp, setting a nearby fuzznik's pants on fire. She bends down to slap the flames and Bucket hip-checks her overboard.

Pirates swarm the remaining planks. No matter how many we knock into the sea, more just keep coming. In seconds, the merchant ship will be overrun.

But then, finally, the sails fill with wind and the merchant vessel pulls away. The gap widens between the ships, sending the planks—and all the pirates on them—into the churning ocean below.

From the *Death Knell*, First Mate Tidepool roars with rage. "Rig the mainsail, lads, and make chase! AND READY THE CANNONS!"

We've escaped, but not for long. The *Death Knell* is a faster ship. It won't take long for them to catch up. And this time they won't bother to board us. They'll just blast us out of the water.

Suddenly a figure leaps from the crow's nest of the *Death Knell*. It soars like a gull and catches one of the ropes of the merchant ship.

I'm about to blast it out of the air with another Magic Missile when I recognize the nimble pirate.

Pan's speaking their language, and they follow her orders without question.

The five of us gather and watch the pirate ship surging through the surf after us. I spot the bedazzler by the ship's wheel. His gemstones glitter menacingly. His huge mouth is locked in a grimace of anger. His one eye glares.

Diremaw the Dread has revenge in his heart. And it is aimed like a cannon. Right at us.

"They'll be on us in no time," I say. Once more, I see my doom approaching. And once more, I'm glad I'm standing with my friends.

"No, they won't," says Pan. "They'll never catch us."

"Why not?" asks Bucket. "Pirate ship is faster."

"Because it's just about six o'clock," she says, pushing back her messy hair.

I'm so confused. "What happens at six o'clock?"

Pan smirks. "Just watch."

The *Death Knell* is so close, I can hear First Mate Tidepool roaring at the crew to open fire.

And that's when it happens.

There is a creaking of breaking timbers. A splitting of wooden planks. The entire pirate ship shudders. The main deck explodes as something huge and leafy bursts from within. The trunk of a gigantic tree.

The *Death Knell* is sinking. The bedazzler looks at his doomed ship. His crew is jumping overboard in

panic. First Mate Tidepool runs to and fro, roaring, "Abandon ship! Abandon ship!"

The bedazzler turn his eye on us. And he shouts, "Enjoy your victory! And know that I will never rest until I have my revenge . . . on the Skullduggery Crew!!!"

With a ship-splintering creak, the tree topples the *Death Knell*, dragging it into the fathomless depths below.

We stand there in awe. Silent. Watching the wreckage disappear into the horizon.

SUPERHEROIC ACHIEVEMENT!
Thwart the Attack of
Diremaw the Dread!
(2,000 Experience Points Awarded)

Moxie gulps. "I wouldn't want to be the Skullduggery Crew about now."

Pan smirks and tugs off her mask. It's the first time I've seen her without it in days. "It's a good thing we're not the Skullduggery Crew," she says. She drops her mask overboard. We all pull off our masks and drop them over the side. They float slowly away on the foamy sea.

For the first time since I've known her, Pan's hair isn't in a tidy topknot. "What did you do?" I ask her. "To the ship?"

She holds up her jade hair clip and pops open the hidden compartment. It's empty.

"A Seed of the Grove," she says, doing her best pixie voice. "Place it within fresh dirt. Water it! And stand back! A mighty titanfrond tree shall spread its roots and grow there and then, bringing the peace of the Sparkly Grove to wherever you are!"

Moxie lets out a howl of laughter. "But where did you find dirt on a pirate ship?"

I nod knowingly. "Ferny."

"Exactly," she says.

"And Cookie always is watering Ferny at exactly six o'clock!" says TickTock with a giggle. "No matter what."

"Exactly," she says.

I look back at the sun setting on the horizon. And I sigh with contentment.

"Gosh, I hate that plant."

CHAPTER THIRTY-SEVEN

The merchants love us.

They shower us with cheers and gold as we enter Wetwater harbor.

Bucket takes a deep, cleansing breath, staring up at the towering twin statues that flank the docks. "Bucket loves this city," he says. "It the one place where Bucket not feel like a monster."

"So?" asks Moxie. "Where to?"

"To the Fried Phoenix," says TickTock wearily. "Tick-Tock is needing a nap."

He's not the only one.

The following week is spent recovering from our adventure on the high seas.

Pan's arm is still weak from the lich's touch but getting stronger each day. And she agrees that we should return to Kevin with his barf. After all, we said we would. After that? Well, we'll see.

Every evening Moxie goes out for a walk by herself. Part of me thinks she's looking for the Skullduggery Crew. And part of me thinks she just needs some alone time. To say goodbye once and for all. To Master Redmane's hammer. And to Master Redmane himself.

Bucket draws lots and lots of pictures.

And me? Well, first I'm super happy to be reunited with my fuzzy bee! But it doesn't last long. The day after we get back, I catch Pan secretively whispering to Bizzy. Bizzy flies away and disappears for several days.

I also study my spellbook. The beginner spells in the front part of the book. If that makes me a baby mage, then I have just one thing to say: *Goo-goo-ga-ga*.

On the morning of our fifth day in Wetwater, Bizzy returns.

"It's time to go," Pan announces.

"Go where?" I ask.

"Back to Kevin's," she says.

"Yes, we is having bedazzler barf to deliver," Tick-Tock agrees.

"But how are we getting back to Kevin?" Moxie asks.

Pan just smirks mysteriously. "You'll see."

We say goodbye to Magda. And we head to the front gates of Wetwater.

"Bucket want to make one stop first," says the ogre.

We follow the ogre through the congested streets. We're not overwhelmed by the crowds anymore. We're the same group that entered Wetwater that first day. But totally different too. We've been to sea. We've faced a lich. I tore apart a shipwreck golem with my bare ten-tacles. We've faced a bedazzler and have the barf to prove it.

As I look at the crowds of strange creatures all around us, I feel something shift inside me.

CONGRATULATIONS!
LEVEL UP!
You are now Level 3!

Bucket stops under the awning of a tattoo shop. A tattooed guy with an orange goatee comes out and greets us. It's the same guy who chased us off his porch on day one.

"Hey there, adventurers," he says. "Name's Clive Quickpen. You guys looking to get inked?"

"No," says Bucket. "Here for this." And he points to a sign in the window.

Clive inspects the little ogre skeptically. "You an artist?"

"Bucket like to draw," Bucket says nervously. He pulls his wrinkled sketch pad from a pocket in his loincloth and offers it to the orange-bearded man.

For several long minutes, Clive looks silently through the pad. His eyes linger on the drawings, carefully considering each page. He finally looks up at the ogre.

"You're very talented," he says. "And that's just what I'm looking for." He smiles a gentle smile. "The job is yours if you want it."

Bucket stands there in awe. "Bucket get paid to draw pictures?"

Clive nods. "Yep."

Bucket turns to Pan, then to me, then to TickTock, and finally to Moxie. "Bucket will stay in Wetwater."

Moxie smiles and wipes a tear from her eye. "We'd love to have you come with us. But—"

Bucket stops her. "Bucket knows. Bucket would not

be welcome most places. But Wetwater is different. Wetwater is good place for Bucket."

Clive places a tattoo-covered arm on the ogre's shoulder. "The job comes with a room over the shop," he says. "You'd have a place to live. And a place for friends to stay when they come to visit."

"Friends," whispers the ogre. Bucket turns to Moxie and grips her in a bear hug. They hold it for a long moment. When the ogre pulls away, he has tears in his eyes.

The ogre reaches out his hand to Clive. Clive shakes it. "Deal!"

This adventure has changed Bucket. Changed me. Changed us all.

Bucket pauses. "Only one thing."

"What's that?" asks Clive.

"Bucket not want to be called Bucket anymore," he says.

"What do you want me to call you?" asks the tattooed man.

He thinks for a minute. Then he smiles and looks at us. "Art," he says. "Art is Bucket's name. Art is Bucket's job."

Clive laughs. "Art it is."

CHAPTER THIRTY-EIGHT

We are outside the gates of Wetwater.

"So?" Moxie turns to Pan curiously. "How are we getting back to Kevin?"

"Are we doing walking?" asks TickTock nervously. "Because TickTock does not want to walk through muck all the way back."

"A little muck isn't so bad, is it?" Pan says. She points to the soggy, sludgy wetlands that sprawl before us.

Waving at us from the muck is Jethro. And Boon-doggle. And Peat Blossom.

"I sent Bizzy with a note," Pan says, shrugging inno-cently. "Seeing if we could hitch a ride with our friends."

I turn to Moxie, and we both bust up laughing.

"Howdy, elf," says Pan, holding out her hand to Peat Blossom.

Peat Blossom looks Pan up and down cautiously. She swats her hand aside. "Get that hand out of my face, princess."

A huge smile splits Peat Blossom's face. She pulls Pan into a hug. "We don't shake hands. We're huggers in these here parts!"

In no time flat, we are saying our goodbyes to the muck elves and knocking at the door of Kevin's tower.

"Dweebs!" cries Kevin in surprise when he opens the door.

"Why do you look so surprised to see us?" Moxie asks as he slaps her on the back.

"I'm not!" he says innocently, leading us inside. "Okay, I am. I totally am. I'm gonna be honest, this was a hard one. I didn't think I would be seeing you again. It made me so sad!"

"Aw," says Moxie.

"I know!" says Kevin. "My breakfast has been a nightmare without TickTock!"

Ah. He didn't miss us or TickTock. He missed runny yolks.

"Hold Kevin's horses," the phibling says. "Hero business first."

Thoughts of eggs vanish. Kevin turns to us, eyes wide. "No! You got it? You didn't get it. Did you get it?"

Moxie opens her pack and pulls out a covered golden urn. "One container of bedazzler barf," she says grandly. "As promised."

Kevin stands before us, speechless. It's a first. I revel in the silence of his mouth not flapping. He takes the urn gently. "How?" he finally sputters. "How did you do it?"

The tale of retrieving the bedazzler barf is long and exciting. Kevin listens appreciatively to our story. He oohs when we tell him about Diremaw being a bedazzler. He aahs when we get to the part about fighting the lich and the shipwreck golem. He gasps when we describe the battle with the pirates and the sinking of the *Death Knell*.

Finally silence settles over him. He looks at us with

wide eyes. And makes the symbol for his brain exploding. "I'm super impressed. You three are turning out to be real hero material."

"Four," Pan says, putting her arm around TickTock.

"That's right," I chime in. "We never would have gotten out of there without his heroism. He's one of us now."

Kevin looks at the beaming phibling skeptically. But he nods. "Yeah, okay. Four."

Pan grips the phibling's shoulder. "Maybe the time has come for you to leave this tower, TickTock."

"Yeah," I say excitedly. "You can come with us!"

"Whoa, whoa, whoa!" objects Kevin. "That's *my* phibling you're trying to steal."

Moxie stands tall against the mage. "TickTock is nobody's phibling. But he is our friend." She turns to the phibling. "It's his decision to make."

TickTock's eyes well up with tears. He chokes back a sob as he looks at each of us. "TickTock loves being with friends. But TickTock thinks he needs a break from adventures for a little while. In Kevin's tower TickTock makes eggs and dusts statues. But TickTock also has his own workshop and freedom to invent and tinker!"

He looks around the room at the tools and work-benches, gadgets and gizmos.

"TickTock is not ready to leave his workshop behind," he says with a smile. "Not yet."

Kevin lets out a huge sigh of relief. "That's more like it! Now, if you weirdos are done trying to lure my best buddy away, I think I owe you some rewards."

He runs over to a large chest and yanks open the lid. "So!" he says. "What's it going to be?"

"TickTock first," says Pan.

TickTock beams proudly. Kevin doesn't look sure that he likes this. But he nods anyway.

"Fine," says Kevin, rummaging through the chest. "I was saving this for your birthday, but now is as good a time as any.

TickTock grabs the box with excitement. "It is being a Build-A-Bot!"

I have no idea what this thing is, but the phibling seems thrilled.

"Those are rare!" says Kevin proudly. "Picked that up in the black markets of Dwarvenforge. Cost me a pretty penny. You're welcome."

But his words are wasted. The phibling is already combing through the box, examining the various gears and gizmos contained within.

Kevin looks Moxie over and begins rummaging through the chest again. "I see you got rid of that old hammer and picked up a shiny new one. How about a magic axe to go with it?"

"No thanks," says Moxie, hefting her silver meat tenderizer. "I've already got a great weapon."

"We'll take cash," says Pan firmly.

"Ooh, yeah," Moxie agrees. "Gold is good!"

"Sheesh! Okay, then!" says Kevin. He pulls a clinking sack out of a drawer and hands it to the elf. "You sound like a monk on a mission."

Pan takes the sack and hefts it, feeling the weight. "We're saving for something."

"You are?" asks Kevin.

"We are?" asks Moxie.

"We are?" I ask.

Pan stares at Kevin. She tucks a couple stray hairwispies behind her ear. And leaves a few out. "We're saving for a ship."

I grin at my elf friend. "A ship, huh?"

"Yeah," she says sheepishly. "A ship. It could be really fun."

"Maybe you're right," I tell her. "After all, we've done a lot of unexpected things. Befriended ogres. Sunk bedazzlers. Smashed a lich to smithereens."

"And don't forget the most unexpected thing of all," Moxie points out. "Pan Silversnow just used the word 'fun'!"

Pan tries to put on a serious face. But a snort of laughter escapes from her.

"That's true," I say, throwing my arm around Pan's shoulders. "Anything could happen next, matey. Anything at all."

The Private Monk Diary of Pan Silversnow

We have accomplished the Great and Powerful Kevin's most recent quest. We have retrieved vomit from a bedazzler.

First a fart. Now a bucket of barf. I cannot begin to guess why he would seek these odd items. Or pay so handsomely for them.

But this I do know.

I do not trust Kevin. Behind his unkempt appearance and impish attitude, there is more to him than meets the eye.

If I had my way, our dealings with him would be at an end.

And yet...

Against my own good judgment, I feel something tugging us back to him. Like a fairy to firelight, as my mother used to say. As though his tower holds some secret that I am meant to discover.

Perhaps it is only morbid curiosity on my part.

Or perhaps something more mysterious is at work here ...

Don't hold your breath for the next Fart Quest!

TURN THE PAGE FOR A SNEAK
PEEK OF BOOK 3. . .

FART QUEST:
THE DRAGON'S DOOKIE

Dropping September 2021

CHAPTER ONE

My head is stuck in a toilet.

Why is my head in a toilet? Two words: water weirdo.

What's a water weirdo? Five words: You don't want to know.

I had never heard of a water weirdo before today. But apparently, the outhouse at the Woozy Wyvern Inn has one. It keeps biting the butts of everyone who uses the facilities. And we've been hired to remove it.

"Are you sure it's still in there?" I ask, pulling my head out of the toilet.

Griff grabs tufts of his hair and tugs in frustration. Griff. Innkeeper of the Woozy Wyvern Inn. And currently, our client.

"Yes, it's in there!" he roars. "Come on, you three! I got customers! I got a reputation to uphold! I gotta do a number two!"

Let's get clear. I'm no stranger to unclogging toilets. When I was an apprentice, I had to do it once a week. Let's just say my master, Elmore the Impressive, had some impressive bowel movements.

But honestly? I thought those days were behind me. I mean, I'm a Level 3 mage, right? I'm an up-and-coming adventurer, right? I'm quickly becoming a heroic figure of myth and legend.

Right?

Nope. I'm a walking, talking potty plunger.

We've tried several things to get this weirdo out of the bathroom. Moxie did her warrior thing.

Apparently, you can't hammer-bash a creature made out of water.

Pan used her monk mojo to water-yank it out.

Didn't work. The water weirdo dived right back into the dumper.

Bizzy, my giant bee, rubs affectionately against my shoulder. I guess it's my turn to dazzle it with magic.

"*Pew-pew-patchoo!*" I shoot a Magic Missile straight down at it. But nada. It just fizzles into the mucky, yucky depths.

Hmm.

I could cast Feather Friend on it. But that only works on birds. Not urine serpents.

I could cast Simple Suggestion on it. But I would have to touch it. And ew.

If only I had an Incantation of Unclogging. But sadly, no.

So here we are. Still stuck with a weirdo in the outhouse.

"Come on, people!" cries Griff. "I'm paying for action! Solutions! Movement!"

"Sometimes the best action is inaction," says Pan.

"Huh?" asks Griff.

"Sometimes the best solution is resolution," says Pan, patting his big ham hand.

Griff does a nervous little holding-it-in jig. "And sometimes the best movement is a bowel movement! Whatever you're going to do, do it quick! Things are getting serious in the land down under!" He turns and flounces back into the inn.

Poor little weirdo. Nobody likes him. Nobody talks to him. He just wants to be left alone in the toilet.

I'm talking about Griff. But yeah, I guess the water weirdo too.

I take another peek down the potty. It must be lonely down there. And then . . . it hits me.

"Maybe we're going about this the wrong way," I suggest.

"Yeah," says Moxie. "Cast something super powerful! What about one of those scrolls Kevin gave you?"

"I only have one left," I tell her. "It's called Stone to String Cheese."

"I can't see that ever coming in handy," mutters Pan, shaking her head.

"You don't know," says Moxie in my defense. "Maybe we'll be starving in a really rocky place. Fart could provide an all-you-can-eat string cheese buffet!"

"We're getting off topic," I say, turning back to the toilet. "What I mean is, maybe we should try using our words instead of our weapons."

"Explain," replies Pan.

"Maybe we should try talking to the water weirdo."

"Interesting," says Pan thoughtfully.

Moxie turns to me. "Can you do that?" she asks. "Can you talk to it?"

I turn to the toilet. And I cast a sweet little spell I've been working on that lets me temporarily talk to any creature. I cast Magic Mouth.

My mom always told me not to talk to weirdos. But this one and I have a nice chat. Turns out, water weirdos are totally reasonable. You just need to find out what they want.

And what this one wants . . . is chicken.

Our client does not seem pleased with our results.

"What do you mean, it's still in there?" roars Griff.

"We made a deal with it," I tell him.

SUPERHEROIC ACHIEVEMENT!
Strike a Bargain with a
Water Weirdo!
(300 Experience Points Awarded)

Griff sighs in defeat. "Fine. What's the deal?"

"It's quite simple," Pan explains. "You feed it one roasted chicken a week, and it agrees to quit biting butts."

We all smile, pleased with our results-oriented approach. "It gets to keep its home and you get to keep your outhouse," I tell him. "It's a fair compromise."

"And if that doesn't work, you could always build another outhouse," Moxie points out. "This place could use another one anyway."

Griff grits his teeth. He grumbles. He gripes. He tells the cook to roast a chicken, and pronto! But he pays us.

SUPERHEROIC ACHIEVEMENT!
Another Satisfied Customer!
(300 Experience Points Awarded)

Sketches for Fart

An artist's process involves lots of exploration. Sometimes it takes a lot of experimenting to make the character look just right!

Sketches for Moxie and Pan

Moxie started out looking too young, so I toughened her up in later versions! I gave her more square shapes in her designs.

Pan never changed. True to her character, she was perfect from the beginning!

Sketches for TickTock

This TickTock looks like he's up to something...

TickTock is a new creature, a balance between man and frog. It's a challenge to illustrate something that hasn't been done before, because I only had the author's text to go with.

Isn't this TickTock cute?!

Want to wield a bo staff like Pan,
swing a hammer like Moxie, or turn someone
into a stinky gas like Fart?

Check out
FART QUEST: THE GAME
to continue the smelly saga with our heroes!

Download it for free at
https://read.macmillan.com/mcpg/fart-quest/

And don't forget! There is
more Fart in your future!

**FART QUEST:
THE DRAGON'S DOOKIE**

Available September 2021

AARON REYNOLDS is a #1 *New York Times*–  bestselling author of many highly acclaimed books for kids, including the Caldecott Honor book *Creepy Carrots!*, *Nerdy Birdy*, *Dude!*, and *The Incredibly Dead Pets of Rex Dexter*. As a longtime Dungeon Master and lover of Dungeons & Dragons, Aaron is no stranger to epic quests. He lives in the Chicago area with his wife, two kids, four cats, and between zero and ten goldfish, depending on the day. **aaron-reynolds.com**

CAM KENDELL is an illustrator of all things absurd  and fantastical; creator of comics such as *Choose Your Gnome Adventure, Mortimer B. Radley: The Case of the Missing Monkey Skull*, and *Flopnar the Bunbarian*; and artist for board games like D&D's Dungeon Mayhem: Monster Madness and 5-Minute Mystery. When not drawing gnomes and/or goblins, Cam enjoys birding, rocking on the accordion, losing at board games, and hiking in the beautiful Utah mountains with his wife and four children, hoping to see a black bear . . . from a safe distance. **camkendell.com**